It was his wife who found him and gave the alarm, so distracted, poor wretch, with fear and horror—for his blood was all over her—that at first the roused household could not make out what she was saying, and thought she had suddenly gone mad. But there, sure enough, at the top of the stairs lay her husband, stone dead, and head foremost, the blood from his wounds dripping down to the steps below him. He had been dreadfully scratched and gashed about the face and throat, as if with curious pointed weapons; and one of his legs had a deep tear in it which had cut an artery, and probably caused his death. But how did he come there, and who had murdered him?

BODIES OF THE DEAD

AND OTHER GREAT AMERICAN GHOST STORIES

EDITED BY
DAVID HARTWELL

A TOM DOHERTY ASSOCIATES BOOK
NEW YORK

BODIES OF THE DEAD AND OTHER GREAT AMERICAN GHOST STORIES

Edited by David Hartwell

All new material Copyright © 1995 by Tom Doherty Associates, Inc.

Cover art by Eric Peterson

A Tor Book
Published by Tom Doherty Associates, Inc.
175 Fifth Avenue
New York, NY 10010

Tor® is a registered trademark of Tom Doherty Associates, Inc.

ISBN: 0-812-54324-6

First edition: August 1995

Printed in the United States of America

0 9 8 7 6 5 4 3 2 1

CONTENTS

KERFOL

Edith Wharton

Y ou ought to buy it," said my host; "it's just the place for a solitary-minded devil like you. And it would be rather worth-while to own the most romantic house in Brittany. The present people are dead broke, and it's going for a song—you ought to buy it."

It was not with the least idea of living up to the character my friend Lanrivain ascribed to me (as a matter of fact, under my unsociable exterior I have always had secret yearnings for domesticity) that I took his hint one autumn afternoon and went to Kerfol. My friend was motoring over to Quimper on business: he dropped me on the way, at a crossroad on a heath, and said: "First turn to the right and second to the left. Then straight ahead till you see an avenue. If you meet any peasants, don't ask your way. They don't understand French, and they would pretend they did and mix you up. I'll be back for you here by sunset—and don't forget the tombs in the chapel."

BODIES OF THE DEAD

I followed Lanrivain's directions with the hesitation occasioned by the usual difficulty of remembering whether he had said the first turn to the right and second to the left, or the contrary. If I had met a peasant I should certainly have asked, and probably been sent astray; but I had the desert landscape to myself, and so stumbled on the right turn and walked across the heath till I came to an avenue. It was so unlike any other avenue I have ever seen that I instantly knew it must be *the* avenue. The grey-trunked trees sprang up straight to a great height and then interwove their pale grey branches in a long tunnel through which the autumn light fell faintly. I know most trees by name, but I haven't to this day been able to decide what those trees were. They had the tall curve of elms, the tenuity of poplars, the ashen color of olives under a rainy sky; and they stretched ahead of me for half a mile or more without a break in their arch. If ever I saw an avenue that unmistakably led to something, it was the avenue at Kerfol. My heart beat a little as I began to walk down it.

Presently the trees ended and I came to a fortified gate in a long wall. Between me and the wall was an open space of grass, with other grey avenues radiating from it. Behind the wall were tall slate roofs mossed with silver, a chapel belfry, the top of a keep. A moat filled with wild shrubs and brambles surrounded the place; the drawbridge had been replaced by a stone arch, and the portcullis by an iron gate. I stood for a long time on the hither side of the moat, gazing about me, and letting the influence of the place sink in. I said to myself: "If I wait long enough, the guardian will turn up and show me the tombs—" and I rather hoped he wouldn't turn up too soon.

I sat down on a stone and lit a cigarette. As soon as I had done it, it struck me as a puerile and portentous

2

thing to do, with that great blind house looking down at me, and all the empty avenues converging on me. It may have been the depth of the silence that made me so conscious of my gesture. The squeak of my match sounded as loud as the scraping of a brake, and I almost fancied I heard it fall when I tossed it onto the grass. But there was more than that: a sense of irrelevance, of littleness, of futile bravado, in sitting there puffing my cigarette smoke into the face of such a past.

I knew nothing of the history of Kerfol—I was new to Brittany, and Lanrivain had never mentioned the name to me till the day before—but one couldn't as much as glance at that pile without feeling in it a long accumulation of history. What kind of history I was not prepared to guess: perhaps only that sheer weight of many associated lives and deaths which gives a majesty to all old houses. But the aspect of Kerfol suggested something more—a perspective of stern and cruel memories stretching away, like its own grey avenues, into a blur of darkness.

Certainly no house had ever more completely and finally broken with the present. As it stood there, lifting its proud roofs and gables to the sky, it might have been its own funeral monument. "Tombs in the chapel? The whole place is a tomb!" I reflected. I hoped more and more that the guardian would not come. The details of the place, however striking, would seem trivial compared with its collective impressiveness; and I wanted only to sit there and be penetrated by the weight of its silence.

"It's the very place for you!" Lanrivain had said; and I was overcome by the almost blasphemous frivolity of suggesting to any living being that Kerfol was the place for him. "Is it possible that anyone could *not* see—?" I wondered. I did not finish the thought: what I meant was undefinable. I stood up and wandered toward the gate. I was beginning to want to know more; not to *see* more—I was by now so sure it was not a question of seeing—but to feel more: feel all the place had to communicate. "But to get in one will have to rout out the keeper," I thought reluctantly, and hesitated. Finally I crossed the bridge and tried the iron gate. It yielded, and I walked through the tunnel formed by the thickness of the *chemin de ronde*. At the farther end, a wooden barricade had been laid across the entrance, and beyond it was a court enclosed in noble architecture. The main building faced me; and I now saw that one-half was a mere ruined front, with gaping windows through which the wild growths of the moat and the trees of the park were visible. The rest of the house was still in its robust beauty. One end abutted on the round tower, the other on the small traceried chapel, and in an angle of the building stood a graceful well-head crowned with mossy urns. A few roses grew against the walls, and on an upper windowsill I remember noticing a pot of fuchsias.

My sense of the pressure of the invisible began to yield to my architectural interest. The building was so fine that I felt a desire to explore it for its own sake. I looked about the court, wondering in which corner the guardian lodged. Then I pushed open the barrier and went in. As I did so, a dog barred my way. He was such a remarkably beautiful little dog that for a moment he made me forget the splendid place he was defending. I was not sure of his breed at the time, but have since learned that it was Chinese, and that he was of a rare variety called the "Sleeve-dog." He was very small and golden brown, with large brown eyes and a ruffled throat: he looked like a large tawny chrysanthemum. I said to myself: "These little beasts always snap and scream, and somebody will be out in a minute."

The little animal stood before me, forbidding, almost menacing: there was anger in his large brown eyes. But he made no sound, he came no nearer. Instead, as I advanced, he gradually fell back, and I noticed that another dog, a vague rough brindled thing, had limped up on a lame leg. "There'll be a hubbub now," I thought; for at the same moment a third dog, a long-haired white mongrel, slipped out of a doorway and joined the others. All three stood looking at me with grave eyes; but not a sound came from them. As I advanced they continued to fall back on muffled paws, still watching me. "At a given point, they'll all charge at my ankles: it's one of the jokes that dogs who live together put up on one," I thought. I was not alarmed, for they were neither large nor formidable. But they let me wander about the court as I pleased, following me at a little distance—always the same distance—and always keeping their eyes on me. Presently I looked across at the ruined façade, and saw that in one of its empty window frames another dog stood: a white pointer with one brown ear. He was an old grave dog, much more experienced than the others; and he seemed to be observing me with a deeper intentness.

"I'll hear from *him*," I said to myself; but he stood in the window frame, against the trees of the park, and continued to watch me without moving. I stared back at him for a time, to see if the sense that he was being watched would not rouse him. Half the width of the court lay between us, and we gazed at each other silently across it. But he did not stir, and at last I turned away. Behind me I found the rest of the pack, with a newcomer added: a small black greyhound with pale agate-colored eyes. He was shivering a little, and his expression was more timid than that of the others. I noticed that he kept a little behind them. And still there was not a sound.

I stood there for fully five minutes, the circle about me—waiting, as they seemed to be waiting. At last I

5

went up to the little golden brown dog and stooped to pat him. As I did so, I heard myself give a nervous laugh. The little dog did not start, or growl, or take his eyes from me—he simply slipped back about a yard, and then paused and continued to look at me. "Oh, hang it!" I exclaimed, and walked across the court toward the well.

As I advanced, the dogs separated and slid away into different corners of the court. I examined the urns on the well, tried a locked door or two, and looked up and down the dumb façade; then I faced about toward the chapel. When I turned I perceived that all the dogs had disappeared except the old pointer, who still watched me from the window. It was rather a relief to be rid of that cloud of witnesses; and I began to look about me for a way to the back of the house. "Perhaps there'll be somebody in the garden," I thought. I found a way across the moat, scrambled over a wall smothered in brambles, and got into the garden. A few lean hydrangeas and geraniums pined in the flower beds, and the ancient house looked down on them indifferently. Its garden side was plainer and severer than the other: the long granite front, with its few windows and steep roof, looked like a fortress prison. I walked around the farther wing, went up some disjointed steps, and entered the deep twilight of a narrow and incredibly old box walk. The walk was just wide enough for one person to slip through, and its branches met overhead. It was like the ghost of a box walk, its lustrous green all turning to the shadowy greyness of the avenues. I walked on and on, the branches hitting me in the face and springing back with a dry rattle; and at length I came out on the grassy top of the *chemin de ronde*. I walked along it to the gate tower, looking down into the court, which was just below me. Not a human being was in sight; and neither were the dogs. I found a flight of steps in the thickness of the wall and went down them; and when I emerged again into the court, there stood the circle of dogs, the golden brown one a little ahead of the others, the black greyhound shivering in the rear.

"Oh, hang it—you uncomfortable beasts, you!" I exclaimed, my voice startling me with a sudden echo. The dogs stood motionless, watching me. I knew by this time that they would not try to prevent my approaching the house, and the knowledge left me free to examine them. I had a feeling that they must be horribly cowed to be so silent and inert. Yet they did not look hungry or ill-treated. Their coats were smooth and they were not thin, except the shivering greyhound. It was more as if they had lived a long time with people who never spoke to them or looked at them: as though the silence of the place had gradually benumbed their busy inquisitive natures. And this strange passivity, this almost human lassitude, seemed to me sadder than the misery of starved and beaten animals. I should have liked to rouse them for a minute, to coax them into a game or a scamper; but the longer I looked into their fixed and weary eyes the more preposterous the idea became. With the windows of that house looking down on us, how could I have imagined such a thing? The dogs knew better: *they* knew what the house would tolerate and what it would not. I even fancied that they knew what was passing through my mind, and pitied me for my frivolity. But even that feeling probably reached them through a thick fog of listlessness. I had an idea that their distance from me was as nothing to my remoteness from them. The impression they produced was that of having in common one memory so deep and dark that nothing that had happened since was worth either a growl or a wag.

"I say," I broke out abruptly, addressing myself to the dumb circle, "do you know what you look like, the

whole lot of you? You look as if you'd seen a ghost—
that's how you look! I wonder if there *is* a ghost here,
and nobody but you left for it to appear to?" The dogs
continued to gaze at me without moving. . . .

It was dark when I saw Lanrivain's motor lamps at the
crossroad—and I wasn't exactly sorry to see them. I had
the sense of having escaped from the loneliest place in
the whole world, and of not liking loneliness—to that
degree—as much as I had imagined I should. My friend
had brought his solicitor back from Quimper for the
night, and seated beside a fat and affable stranger I felt
no inclination to talk of Kerfol. . . .

But that evening, when Lanrivain and the solicitor
were closeted in the study, Madame de Lanrivain began
to question me in the drawing room.

"Well—are you going to buy Kerfol?" she asked, tilt-
ing up her gay chin from her embroidery.

"I haven't decided yet. The fact is, I couldn't get into
the house," I said, as if I had simply postponed my decision, and meant to go back for another look.

"You couldn't get in? Why, what happened? The
family are mad to sell the place, and the old guardian
has orders—"

"Very likely. But the old guardian wasn't there."

"What a pity! He must have gone to market. But his
daughter—?"

"There was nobody about. At least I saw no one."

"How extraordinary! Literally nobody?"

"Nobody but a lot of dogs—a whole pack of them—
who seemed to have the place to themselves."

Madame de Lanrivain let the embroidery slip to her
knee and folded her hands on it. For several minutes
she looked at me thoughtfully.

"A pack of dogs—you *saw* them?"

"Saw them? I saw nothing else!"

8

"How many?" She dropped her voice a little. "I've always wondered—"

I looked at her with surprise: I had supposed the place to be familiar to her. "Have you never been to Kerfol?" I asked.

"Oh, yes: often. But never on that day."

"What day?"

"I'd quite forgotten—and so had Hervé, I'm sure. If we'd remembered, we never should have sent you today—but then, after all, one doesn't half believe that sort of thing, does one?"

"What sort of thing?" I asked, involuntarily sinking my voice to the level of hers. Inwardly I was thinking: "I *knew* there was something. . . ."

Madame de Lanrivain cleared her throat and produced a reassuring smile. "Didn't Hervé tell you the story of Kerfol? An ancestor of his was mixed up in it. You know every Breton house has its ghost story; and some of them are rather unpleasant."

"Yes—but those dogs?"

"Well, those dogs are the ghosts of Kerfol. At least, the peasants say there's one day in the year when a lot of dogs appear there; and that day the keeper and his daughter go off to Morlaix and get drunk. The women in Brittany drink dreadfully." She stooped to match a silk; then she lifted her charming inquisitive Parisian face. "Did you *really* see a lot of dogs? There isn't one at Kerfol," she said.

· II ·

Lanrivain, the next day, hunted out a shabby calf volume from the back of an upper shelf of his library.

"Yes—here it is. What does it call itself? *A History of the Assizes of the Duchy of Brittany. Quimper, 1702.*

BODIES OF THE DEAD

The book was written about a hundred years later than the Kerfol affair; but I believe the account is transcribed pretty literally from the judicial records. Anyhow, it's queer reading. And there's a Hervé de Lanrivain mixed up in it—not exactly *my* style, as you'll see. But then he's only a collateral. Here, take the book up to bed with you. I don't exactly remember the details; but after you've read it I'll bet anything you'll leave your light burning all night!"

I left my light burning all night, as he had predicted; but it was chiefly because, till near dawn, I was absorbed in my reading. The account of the trial of Anne de Cornault, wife of the lord of Kerfol, was long and closely printed. It was, as my friend had said, probably an almost literal transcription of what took place in the courtroom; and the trial lasted nearly a month. Besides, the type of the book was very bad. . . .

At first I thought of translating the old record. But it is full of wearisome repetitions, and the main lines of the story are forever straying off into side issues. So I have tried to disentangle it, and give it here in a simpler form. At times, however, I have reverted to the text because no other words could have been conveyed so exactly the sense of what I felt at Kerfol; and nowhere have I added anything of my own.

· III ·

It was in the year 16— that Yves de Cornault, lord of the domain of Kerfol, went to the *pardon* of Locronan to perform his religious duties. He was a rich and powerful noble, then in his sixty-second year, but hale and sturdy, a great horseman and hunter and a pious man. So all his neighbors attested. In appearance he was short and broad, with a swarthy face, legs slightly

10

bowed from the saddle, a hanging nose and broad hands
with black hairs on them. He had married young and
lost his wife and son soon after, and since then had
lived alone at Kerfol. Twice a year he went to Morlaix,
where he had a handsome house by the river, and spent
a week or ten days there; and occasionally he rode to
Rennes on business. Witnesses were found to declare
that during these absences he led a life different from
the one he was known to lead at Kerfol, where he
busied himself with his estate, attended mass daily, and
found his only amusement in hunting the wild boar and
waterfowl. But these rumors are not particularly rele-
vant, and it is certain that among people of his own
class in the neighborhood he passed for a stern and even
austere man, observant of his religious obligations, and
keeping strictly to himself. There was no talk of any fa-
miliarity with the women on his estate, though at that
time the nobility were very free with their peasants.
Some people said he had never looked at a woman
since his wife's death; but such things are hard to prove,
and the evidence on this point was not worth much.

Well, in his sixty-second year, Yves de Cornault went
to the *pardon* at Locronan, and saw there a young lady
of Douarnenez, who had ridden over pillion behind her
father to do her duty to the saint. Her name was Anne
de Barrigan, and she came of good old Breton stock,
but much less great and powerful than that of Yves de
Cornault; and her father had squandered his fortune at
cards, and lived almost like a peasant in his little granite
manor on the moors. . . . I have said I would add nothing of my own to this bald statement of a strange case;
but I must interrupt myself here to describe the young
lady who rode up to the lych-gate of Locronan at the
very moment when the Baron de Cornault was also dis-
mounting there. I take my description from a faded
drawing in red crayon, sober and truthful enough to be

11

by a late pupil of the Clouets, which hangs in Lanrivain's study, and is said to be a portrait of Anne de Barrigan. It is unsigned and has no mark of identity but the initials A. B., and the date 16—, the year after her marriage. It represents a young woman with a small oval face, almost pointed, yet wide enough for a full mouth with a tender depression at the corners. The nose is small, and the eyebrows are set rather high, far apart, and as lightly penciled as the eyebrows in a Chinese painting. The forehead is high and serious, and the hair, which one feels to be fine and thick and fair, is drawn off it and lies close like a cap. The eyes are neither large nor small, hazel probably, with a look at once shy and steady. A pair of beautiful long hands are crossed below the lady's breast. . . .

The chaplain of Kerfol, and other witnesses, averred that when the Baron came back from Locronan he jumped from his horse, ordered another to be instantly saddled, called to a young page to come with him, and rode away that same evening to the south. His steward followed the next morning with coffers laden on a pair of pack mules. The following week Yves de Cornault rode back to Kerfol, sent for his vassals and tenants, and told them he was to be married at All Saints to Anne de Barrigan of Douarnenez. And on All Saints' Day the marriage took place.

As to the next few years, the evidence on both sides seems to show that they passed happily for the couple. No one was found to say that Yves de Cornault had been unkind to his wife, and it was plain to all that he was content with his bargain. Indeed, it was admitted by the chaplain and other witnesses for the prosecution that the young lady had a softening influence on her husband, and that he became less exacting with his tenants, less harsh to peasants and dependents, and less subject to the fits of gloomy silence which had darkened his widowhood. As to his wife, the only grievance her champions could call up in her behalf was that Kerfol was a lonely place, and that when her husband was away on business at Rennes or Morlaix—whither she was never taken—she was not allowed so much as to walk in the park unaccompanied. But no one asserted that she was unhappy, though one servant woman said she had surprised her crying, and had heard her say that she was a woman accursed to have no child, and nothing in life to call her own. But that was a natural enough feeling in a wife attached to her husband; and certainly it must have been a great grief to Yves de Cornault that she bore no son. Yet he never made her feel her childlessness as a reproach—she admits this in her evidence—but seemed to try to make her forget it by showering gifts and favors on her. Rich though he was, he had never been openhanded; but nothing was too fine for his wife, in the way of silks or gems or linen, or whatever else she fancied. Every wandering merchant was welcome at Kerfol, and when the master was called away he never came back without bringing his wife a handsome present—something curious and particular—from Morlaix or Rennes or Quimper. One of the waiting women gave, in cross-examination, an interesting list of one year's gifts, which I copy. From Morlaix, a carved ivory junk, with Chinamen at the oars, that a strange sailor had brought back as a votive offering for Notre Dame de la Clarté, above Ploumanac'h; from Quimper, an embroidered gown, worked by the nuns of the Assumption; from Rennes, a silver rose that opened and showed an amber Virgin with a crown of garnets; from Morlaix, again, a length of Damascus velvet shot with gold, bought of a Jew from Syria; and for Michaelmas that same year, from Rennes a necklet or bracelet of round stones—emeralds and pearls and rubies—strung like beads on a fine gold chain. This was the present that pleased the lady best, the woman said. Later on, as it happened, it was produced at the trial, and appears to have struck the Judges and the public as a curious and valuable jewel.

The very same winter, the Baron absented himself again, this time as far as Bordeaux, and on his return he brought his wife something even odder and prettier than the bracelet. It was a winter evening when he rode up to Kerfol and, walking into the hall, found her sitting by the hearth, her chin on her hand, looking into the fire. He carried a velvet box in his hand and, setting it down, lifted the lid and let out a little golden brown dog.

Anne de Cornault exclaimed with pleasure as the little creature bounded toward her. "Oh, it looks like a bird or a butterfly!" she cried as she picked it up; and the dog put its paws on her shoulders and looked at her with eyes "like a Christian's." After that she would never have it out of her sight, and petted and talked to it as if it had been a child— As indeed it was the nearest thing to a child she was to know. Yves de Cornault was much pleased with his purchase. The dog had been brought to him by a sailor from an East India merchantman, and the sailor had bought it of a pilgrim in a bazaar at Jaffa, who had stolen it from a nobleman's wife in China: a perfectly permissible thing to do, since the pilgrim was a Christian and the nobleman a heathen doomed to hell-fire. Yves de Cornault had paid a long price for the dog, for they were beginning to be in demand at the French court, and the sailor knew he had got hold of a good thing; but Anne's pleasure was so great that, to see her laugh and play with the little animal, her husband would doubtless have given twice the sum.

So far, all the evidence is at one, and the narrative plain sailing; but now the steering becomes difficult. I will try to keep as nearly as possible to Anne's own statements, though toward the end, poor thing. . . .

Well, to go back. The very year after the little brown dog was brought to Kerfol, Yves de Cornault, one winter night, was found dead at the head of a narrow flight of stairs leading down from his wife's rooms to a door opening on the court. It was his wife who found him and gave the alarm, so distracted, poor wretch, with fear and horror—for his blood was all over her—that at first the roused household could not make out what she was saying, and thought she had suddenly gone mad. But there, sure enough, at the top of the stairs lay her husband, stone dead, and head foremost, the blood from his wounds dripping down to the steps below him. He had been dreadfully scratched and gashed about the face and throat, as if with curious pointed weapons; and one of his legs had a deep tear in it which had cut an artery, and probably caused his death. But how did he come there, and who had murdered him?

His wife declared that she had been asleep in her bed, and hearing his cry had rushed out to find him lying on the stairs; but this was immediately questioned. In the first place, it was proved that from her room she could not have heard the struggle on the stairs, owing to the thickness of the walls and the length of the intervening passage; then it was evident that she had not been in bed and asleep, since she was dressed when she roused the house, and her bed had not been slept in. Moreover, the door at the bottom of the stairs was ajar, and it was noticed by the chaplain (an observant man) that the dress she wore was stained with blood about the knees, and that there were traces of small bloodstained hands low down on the staircase walls, so that it was conjectured that she had really been at the postern door when her husband fell and, feeling her way up to him in the darkness on her hands and knees, had been stained by his blood dripping down on her. Of course it was argued on the other side that the blood marks on her dress might have been caused by her kneeling down by her husband when she rushed out of her room; but there was the open door below, and the fact that the finger marks in the staircase all pointed upward.

The accused held to her statement for the first two days, in spite of its improbability; but on the third day word was brought to her that Hervé de Lanrivain, a young nobleman of the neighborhood, had been arrested for complicity in the crime. Two or three witnesses thereupon came forward to say that it was known throughout the country that Lanrivain had formerly been on good terms with the lady of Cornault; but that he had been absent from Brittany for over a year, and people had ceased to associate their names. The witnesses who made this statement were not of a very reputable sort. One was an old herb-gatherer suspected of witchcraft, another a drunken clerk from a neighboring parish, the third a half-witted shepherd who could be made to say anything; and it was clear that the prosecution was not satisfied with its case, and would have liked to find more definite proof of Lanrivain's complicity than the statement of the herb-gatherer, who swore to having seen him climbing the wall of the park on the night of the murder. One way of patching out incomplete proofs in those days was to put some sort of pressure, moral or physical, on the accused person. It is not clear what pressure was put on Anne de Cornault; but on the third day, when she was brought in court, she "appeared weak and wandering," and after being encouraged to collect herself and speak the truth, on her honor and the wounds of her Blessed Redeemer, she confessed that she had in fact gone down the stairs to speak with Hervé de Lanrivain (who denied everything), and had been surprised there by the sound of her husband's fall. That was better; and the prosecution rubbed its hands with satisfaction. The satisfaction increased when various dependents living at Kerfol were induced to say—with apparent sincerity—that during the year or two preceding his death their master had once more grown uncertain and irascible, and subject to the fits of brooding silence which his household had learned to dread before his second marriage. This seemed to show that things had not been going well at Kerfol; though no one could be found to say that there had been any signs of open disagreement between husband and wife.

Anne de Cornault, when questioned as to her reason for going down at night to open the door to Hervé de Lanrivain, made an answer which must have sent a smile around the court. She said it was because she was lonely and wanted to talk with the young man. Was this the only reason? she was asked; and replied: "Yes, by the Cross over your Lordships' heads." "But why at midnight?" the court asked. "Because I could see him in no other way." I can see the exchange of glances across the ermine collars under the Crucifix.

Anne de Cornault, further questioned, said that her married life had been extremely lonely: "desolate" was the word she used. It was true that her husband seldom spoke harshly to her; but there were days when he did not speak at all. It was true that he had never struck or threatened her; but he kept her like a prisoner at Kerfol, and when he rode away to Morlaix or Quimper or Rennes he set so close a watch on her that she could not pick a flower in the garden without having a waiting woman at her heels. "I am no Queen, to need such honors," she once said to him; and he had answered that a man who has a treasure does not leave the key in the lock when he goes out. "Then take me with you," she urged; but to this he said that towns were pernicious places, and young wives better off at their own fire-sides.

"But what did you want to say to Hervé de Lanrivain?" the court asked; and she answered: "To ask him to take me away."

"Ah—you confess that you went down to him with adulterous thoughts?"

"No."

"Then why did you want him to take you away?"

"Because I was afraid for my life."

"Of whom were you afraid?"

"Of my husband."

"Why were you afraid of your husband?"

"Because he had strangled my little dog."

Another smile must have passed around the courtroom: in days when any nobleman had a right to hang his peasants—and most of them exercised it—pinching a pet animal's windpipe was nothing to make a fuss about.

At this point one of the Judges, who appears to have had a certain sympathy for the accused, suggested that she should be allowed to explain herself in her own way; and she thereupon made the following statement.

The first years of her marriage had been lonely; but her husband had not been unkind to her. If she had had a child she would not have been unhappy; but the days were long, and it rained too much.

It was true that her husband, whenever he went away and left her, brought her a handsome present on his return; but this did not make up for the loneliness. At least nothing had, till he brought her the little brown dog from the East: after that she was much less unhappy. Her husband seemed pleased that she was so fond of the dog; he gave her leave to put her jeweled bracelet around its neck, and to keep it always with her.

One day she had fallen asleep in her room, with the

dog at her feet, as his habit was. Her feet were bare and resting on his back. Suddenly she was waked by her husband: he stood beside her, smiling not unkindly.

"You look like my great-grandmother, Juliane de Cornault, lying in the chapel with her feet on a little dog," he said.

The analogy sent a chill through her, but she laughed and answered: "Well, when I am dead you must put me beside her, carved in marble, with my dog at my feet."

"Oho—we'll wait and see," he said, laughing also, but with his black brows close together. "The dog is the emblem of fidelity."

"And do you doubt my right to lie with mine at my feet?"

"When I'm in doubt I find out," he answered. "I am an old man," he added, "and people say I make you lead a lonely life. But I swear you shall have your monument if you earn it."

"And I swear to be faithful," she returned, "if only for the sake of having my little dog at my feet."

Not long afterward he went on business to the Quimper Assizes; and while he was away his aunt, the widow of a great nobleman of the duchy, came to spend a night at Kerfol on her way to the *pardon* of Ste. Barbe. She was a woman of piety and consequence, and much respected by Yves de Cornault, and when she proposed to Anne to go with her to Ste. Barbe no one could object, and even the chaplain declared himself in favor of the pilgrimage. So Anne set out for Ste. Barbe, and there for the first time she talked with Hervé de Lanrivain. He had come once or twice to Kerfol with his father, but she had never before exchanged a dozen words with him. They did not talk for more than five minutes now: it was under the chestnuts, as the procession was coming out of the chapel. He said: "I pity you," and she was surprised, for she had not supposed that anyone thought her an object of pity. He added: "Call for me when you need me," and she smiled a little, but was glad afterward, and thought often of the meeting.

She confessed to having seen him three times afterward: not more. How or where she would not say—one had the impression that she feared to implicate someone. Their meetings had been rare and brief; and at the last he had told her that he was starting the next day for a foreign country, on a mission which was not without peril and might keep him for many months absent. He asked her for a remembrance, and she had none to give him but the collar about the little dog's neck. She was sorry afterward that she had given it, but he was so unhappy at going that she had not had the courage to refuse.

Her husband was away at the time. When he returned a few days later he picked up the animal to pet it, and noticed that its collar was missing. His wife told him that the dog had lost it in the undergrowth of the park, and that she and her maids had hunted a whole day for it. It was true, she explained to the court, that she had made the maids search for the necklet—they all believed the dog had lost it in the park. : ...

Her husband made no comment, and that evening at supper he was in his usual mood, between good and bad: you could never tell which. He talked a good deal, describing what he had seen and done at Rennes; but now and then he stopped and looked hard at her, and when she went to bed she found her little dog strangled on her pillow. The little thing was dead, but still warm; she stopped to lift it, and her distress turned to horror when she discovered that it had been strangled by twisting twice round its throat the necklet she had given to Lanrivain.

The next morning at dawn she buried the dog in the garden, and hid the necklet in her breast. She said nothing to her husband, then or later, and he said nothing to her; but that day he had a peasant hanged for stealing a faggot in the park, and the next day he nearly beat to death a young horse he was breaking.

Winter set in, and the short days passed, and the long nights, one by one; and she heard nothing of Hervé de Lanrivain. It might be that her husband had killed him; or merely that he had been robbed of the necklet. Day after day by the hearth among the spinning maids, night after night alone on her bed, she wondered and trembled. Sometimes at table her husband looked across at her and smiled; and then she felt sure that Lanrivain was dead. She dared not try to get news of him, for she was sure her husband would find out if she did: she had an idea that he could find out anything. Even when a witch woman who was a noted seer, and could show you the whole world in her crystal, came to the castle for a night's shelter, and the maids flocked to her, Anne held back.

The winter was long and black and rainy. One day, in Yves de Cornault's absence, some gypsies came to Kerfol with a troop of performing dogs. Anne bought the smallest and cleverest, a white dog with a feathery coat and one blue and one brown eye. It seemed to have been ill-treated by the gypsies, and clung to her plaintively when she took it from them. That evening her husband came back, and when she went to bed she found the dog strangled on her pillow.

After that she said to herself that she would never have another dog; but one bitter cold evening a poor lean greyhound was found whining at the castle gate, and she took him in and forbade the maids to speak of him to her husband. She hid him in a room that no one went to, smuggled food to him from her own plate, made him a warm bed to lie on and petted him like a child.

Yves de Cornault came home, and the next day she found the greyhound strangled on her pillow. She wept in secret, but said nothing, and resolved that even if she met a dog dying of hunger she would never bring him into the castle; but one day she found a young sheep dog, a brindled puppy with good blue eyes, lying with a broken leg in the snow of the park. Yves de Cornault was at Rennes, and she brought the dog in, warmed and fed it, tied up its leg and hid it in the castle till her husband's return. The day before, she gave it to a peasant woman who lived a long way off, and paid her handsomely to care for it and say nothing; but that night she heard a whining and scratching at her door, and when she opened it the lame puppy, drenched and shivering, jumped up on her with little sobbing barks. She hid him in her bed, and the next morning was about to have him taken back to the peasant woman when she heard her husband ride into the court. She shut the dog in a chest, and went down to receive him. An hour later, when she returned to her room, the puppy lay strangled on her pillow. . . .

After that she dared not make a pet of any other dog; and her loneliness became almost unendurable. Sometimes, when she crossed the court of the castle, and thought no one was looking, she stopped to pat the old pointer at the gate. But one day as she was caressing him her husband came out of the chapel; and the next day the old dog was gone. . . .

This curious narrative was not told in one sitting of the court, or received without impatience and incredulous comment. It was plain that the Judges were surprised by its puerility, and that it did not help the accused in the eyes of the public. It was an odd tale, certainly; but what did it prove? That Yves de Cornault disliked dogs, and that his wife, to gratify her own fancy, persistently ignored this dislike. As for pleading this trivial disagreement as an excuse for her relations— whatever their nature—with her supposed accomplice, the argument was so absurd that her own lawyer manifestly regretted having let her make use of it, and tried several times to cut short her story. But she went on to the end, with a kind of hypnotized insistence, as though the scenes she evoked were so real to her that she had forgotten where she was and imagined herself to be reliving them.

At length the Judge who had previously shown a certain kindness to her said (leaning forward a little, one may suppose, from his row of dozing colleagues): "Then you would have us believe that you murdered your husband because he would not let you keep a pet dog?"

"I did not murder my husband."

"Who did, then? Hervé de Lanrivain?"

"No."

"Who then? Can you tell us?"

"Yes, I can tell you. The dogs—" At that point she was carried out of the court in a swoon.

It was evident that her lawyer tried to get her to abandon this line of defense. Possibly her explanation, whatever it was, had seemed convincing when she poured it out to him in the heat of their first private colloquy; but now that it was exposed to the cold daylight of judicial scrutiny, and the banter of the town, he was thoroughly ashamed of it, and would have sacrificed her without a scruple to save his professional reputation. But the obstinate Judge—who perhaps, after all, was more inquisitive than kindly—evidently wanted to hear the story out, and she was ordered, the next day, to continue her deposition.

She said that after the disappearance of the old

watchdog nothing particular happened for a month or two. Her husband was much as usual: she did not remember any special incident. But one evening a peddler woman came to the castle and was selling trinkets to the maids. She had no heart for trinkets, but she stood looking on while the women made their choice. And then, she did not know how, but the peddler coaxed her into buying for herself a pear-shaped pomander with a strong scent in it—she had once seen something of the kind on a gypsy woman. She had no desire for the pomander, and did not know why she had bought it. The peddler said that whoever wore it had the power to read the future; but she did not really believe that, or care much either. However, she bought the thing and took it up to her room, where she sat turning it about in her hand. Then the strange scent attracted her and she began to wonder what kind of spice was in the box. She opened it and found a grey bean rolled in a strip of paper; and on the paper she saw a sign she knew, and a message from Hervé de Lanrivain, saying that he was at home again and would be at the door in the court that night after the moon had set. . . .

She burned the paper and set down to think. It was nightfall, and her husband was at home. . . . She had no way of warning Lanrivain, and there was nothing to do but to wait. . . .

At this point I fancy the drowsy courtroom beginning to wake up. Even to the oldest hand on the bench there must have been a certain relish in picturing the feelings of a woman on receiving such a message at nightfall from a man living twenty miles away, to whom she had no means of sending a warning. . . .

She was not a clever woman, I imagine; and as the first result of her cogitation she appears to have made the mistake of being, that evening, too kind to her husband. She could not ply him with wine, according to the traditional expedient, for though he drank heavily at times he had a strong head; and when he drank beyond its strength it was because he chose to, and not because a woman coaxed him. Not his wife, at any rate—she was an old story by now. As I read the case, I fancy there was no feeling for her left in him but the hatred occasioned by his supposed dishonor.

At any rate, she tried to call up her old graces; but early in the evening he complained of pains and fever, and left the hall to go up to the closet where he sometimes slept. His servant carried him a cup of hot wine, and brought back word that he was sleeping and not to be disturbed; and an hour later, when Anne lifted the tapestry and listened at his door, she heard his loud regular breathing. She thought it might be a feint, and stayed a long time barefooted in the passage, her ear to the crack; but the breathing went on too steadily and naturally to be other than that of a man in a sound sleep. She crept back to her room reassured, and stood in the window watching the moon set through the trees of the park. The sky was misty and starless, and after the moon went down the night was black as pitch. She knew the time had come, and stole along the passage, past her husband's door—where she stopped again to listen to his breathing—to the top of the stairs. There she paused a moment, and assured herself that no one was following her; then she began to go down the stairs in the darkness. They were so steep and winding that she had to go very slowly, for fear of stumbling. Her one thought was to get the door unbolted, tell Lanrivain to make his escape, and hasten back to her room. She had tried the bolt earlier in the evening, and managed to put a little grease on it; but nevertheless, when she drew it, it gave a squeak ... not loud, but it made her heart stop; and the next minute, overhead, she heard a noise. . . .

"What noise?" the prosecution interposed.

"My husband's voice calling out my name and cursing me."

"What did you hear after that?"

"A terrible scream and a fall."

"Where was Hervé de Lanrivain at this time?"

"He was standing outside in the court. I just made him out in the darkness. I told him for God's sake to go, and then I pushed the door shut."

"What did you do next?"

"I stood at the foot of the stairs and listened."

"What did you hear?"

"I heard dogs snarling and panting." (Visible discouragement of the bench, boredom of the public, and exasperation of the lawyer for the defense. Dogs again—! But the inquisitive Judge insisted.)

"What dogs?"

She bent her head and spoke so low that she had to be told to repeat her answer: "I don't know."

"How do you mean—you don't know?"

"I don't know what dogs. . . ."

The Judge again intervened: "Try to tell us exactly what happened. How long did you remain at the foot of the stairs?"

"Only a few minutes."

"And what was going on meanwhile overhead?"

"The dogs kept on snarling and panting. Once or twice he cried out. I think he moaned once. Then he was quiet."

"Then what happened?"

"Then I heard a sound like the noise of a pack when the wolf is thrown to them—gulping and lapping."

(There was a groan of disgust and repulsion through

the court, and another attempted intervention by the distracted lawyer. But the inquisitive Judge was still inquisitive.)

"And all the while you did not go up?"

"Yes—I went up then—to drive them off."

"The dogs?"

"Yes."

"Well—?"

"When I got there it was quite dark. I found my husband's flint and steel and struck a spark. I saw him lying there. He was dead."

"And the dogs?"

"The dogs were gone."

"Gone—where to?"

"I don't know. There was no way out—and there were no dogs at Kerfol."

She straightened herself to her full height, threw her arms above her head, and fell down on the stone floor with a long scream. There was a moment of confusion in the courtroom. Someone on the bench was heard to say: "This is clearly a case for the ecclesiastical authorities"—and the prisoner's lawyer doubtless jumped at the suggestion.

After this, the trial loses itself in a maze of cross-questioning and squabbling. Every witness who was called corroborated Anne de Cornault's statement that there were no dogs at Kerfol: had been none for several months. The master of the house had taken a dislike to dogs, there was no denying it. But, on the other hand, at the inquest, there had been long and bitter discussions as to the nature of the dead man's wounds. One of the surgeons called in had spoken of marks that looked like bites. The suggestion of witchcraft was revived, and the opposing lawyers hurled tomes of necromancy at each other.

At last Anne de Cornault was brought back into court—at the instance of the same Judge—and asked if she knew where the dogs she spoke of could have come from. On the body of her Redeemer she swore that she did not. Then the Judge put his final question: "If the dogs you think you heard had been known to you, do you think you would have recognized them by their barking?"

"Yes."

"Did you recognize them?"

"Yes."

"What dogs do you take them to have been?"

"My dead dogs," she said in a whisper. . . . She was taken out of court, not to reappear there again. There was some kind of ecclesiastical investigation, and the end of the business was that the Judges disagreed with each other, and with the ecclesiastical committee, and that Anne de Cornault was finally handed over to the keeping of her husband's family, who shut her up in the keep of Kerfol, where she is said to have died many years later, a harmless madwoman.

So ends her story. As for that of Hervé de Lanrivain, I had only to apply to his collateral descendant for its subsequent details. The evidence against the young man being insufficient, and his family influence in the duchy considerable, he was set free, and left soon afterward for Paris. He was probably in no mood for a worldly life, and he appears to have come almost immediately under the influence of the famous M. Arnauld d'Andilly and the gentlemen of Port Royal. A year or two later he was received into their Order, and without achieving any particular distinction he followed its good and evil fortunes till his death some twenty years later. Lanrivain showed me a portrait of him by a pupil of Philippe de Champaigne: sad eyes, an impulsive mouth and a narrow brow. Poor Hervé de Lanrivain: it was a grey ending. Yet as I looked at his stiff and sallow effigy, in the dark dress of the Jansenists, I almost found myself envying his fate. After all, in the course of his life two great things had happened to him: he had loved romantically, and he must have talked with Pascal. . . .

THE INTOXICATED GHOST

Arlo Bates

I

It was not her beauty which made Irene Gaspic unusual, although she was bewitchingly pretty; nor yet her wit, her cleverness, or her wealth, albeit she was well endowed with all these good gifts: other girls were pretty, and wise, and witty, and rich. It was something far more piquant and rare which marked Irene as different from her mates, the fact being that from her great-aunt on the mother's side, an old lady who for nearly ninety years displayed to her fellow-mortals one of the most singular characters possible, Irene had inherited the power of seeing ghosts.

It is so generally regarded as a weakness even to believe in disembodied spirits that in justice to Irene it is but fair to remark that she believed in them only because she could not help seeing them, and that the power with which she was endowed had come to her by inheritance quite without any wish on her part. Any fair-minded person must perceive the difference between seeing ghosts because one is so foolish as to believe in them, and believing in their existence because one cannot help seeing them. It might be added, moreover, that the firmness which Miss Gaspic had displayed when visited by some of the most unpleasant wraiths in the whole category should be allowed to tell in her favor. When she was approached during a visit to Castle Doddyfoethghw—where, as every traveler in Wales is aware, is to be found the most ghostly phantom in the three kingdoms—by a gory figure literally streaming with blood, and carrying its mangled head in its hands, she merely remarked coldly: "Go away at once, please. You do not alarm me in the least; but to come into the presence of a lady in such a state of unpleasant dismemberment is in shockingly bad taste." Whereat the poor wraith fell all along the ground in astonishment and alarm, leaving a stain of blood upon the stone floor, which may be seen to this day by any one who doubts the tale enough to go to Castle Doddyfoethghw to see.

Although Irene seldom referred to her inheritance, and professed, when she did speak of it, to feel a lively indignation that her aunt Eunice Mariamne should have thrust upon her such a bequest, she was too thoroughly human and feminine to lack wholly a secret pride that she should be distinguished by a gift so unusual. She had too good taste openly to talk of it, yet she had not the firmness entirely to conceal it; and her friends were pretty generally aware of the legacy and of many circumstances resulting from its possession. Some few of her intimates, indeed, had ventured to employ her good offices in communicating with family wraiths; and although Irene was averse to anything which savored so strongly of mediumship and other vulgar trades, she could not but be pleased at the excellent results which had followed her mediations in several instances.

When, therefore, she one day received a note from her old school friend Fanny McHugh, inviting her to come down to visit her at Oldtower, with the mysterious remark, "I not only long to see you, dear, but there is something most important that you can do for me, and nobody but you," Irene at once remembered that the McHughs had a family ghost, and was convinced that she was invited, so to say, in her professional capacity.

She was, however, by no means averse to going, and that for several reasons. The McHugh estate was a beautiful old place in one of the loveliest of New England villages, where the family had been in the ascendancy since pre-Revolutionary days; Irene was sufficiently fond of Fanny; and she was well aware, in virtue of that intuition which enables women to know so many things, that her friend's brother, Arthur McHugh, would be at home at the time named for the visit. Irene and Lieutenant Arthur McHugh had been so much to each other at one time that they had been to the very verge of a formal engagement, when at the last moment he drew back. There was no doubt of his affection, but he was restrained from asking Irene to share his fortunes by the unpleasant though timely remembrance that he had none. The family wealth, once princely for the country and time, had dwindled until little remained save the ancestral mansion and the beautiful but unremunerative lawns surrounding it.

Of course this conduct upon the part of Lieutenant McHugh was precisely that which most surely fixed him in the heart of Irene. The lover who continues to love, but unselfishly renounces, is hardly likely to be forgotten; and it is to be presumed that it was with more thought of the young and handsome lieutenant in flesh and blood than of the Continental major in ghostly attenuation who lurked in the haunted chamber that Miss Gaspic accepted the invitation to Oldtower.

II

Oldtower stands in a wild and beautiful village, left on one side by modern travel, which has turned away from the turnpike of the fathers to follow the more direct route of the rail. The estate extends for some distance along the bank of the river, which so twists in its windings as almost to make the village an island, and on a knoll overlooking the stream moulders the crumbling pile of stone which once was a watch-tower, and from which the place takes its name.

The house is one of the finest of old colonial mansions, and is beautifully placed upon a terrace half a dozen feet above the level of the ample lawn which surrounds it. Back of the house a trim garden with box hedges as high as the gardener's knee extends down to the river, while in front a lofty hedge shuts off the grounds from the village street. Miss Fanny, upon whom had largely devolved the care of the estate since the death of her widowed mother, had had the good sense to confine her efforts to keeping things in good order in the simplest possible way; and the result was that such defects of management as were rendered inevitable by the smallness in income presented themselves to the eye rather as evidences of mellowness than of decay, and the general effect remained most charming.

Irene had always been fond of the McHugh place, and everything was in the perfection of its June fairness when she arrived. Her meeting with Fanny was properly effusive, while Arthur gratified her feminine sense by greeting her with outward calmness while he allowed his old passion to appear in his eyes. There were, of course, innumerable questions to be asked, as is usual upon such occasions, and some of them were even of sufficient importance to require answers; so that the afternoon passed rapidly away, and Irene had no opportunity to refer to the favor to which her friend's letter had made allusion. Her suspicion that she had been summoned in her capacity of ghost-seer was confirmed by the fact that she had been put in the haunted room, a fine square chamber in the southeast wing, wainscoted to the ceiling, and one of the handsomest apartments in the house. This room had been especially decorated and fitted up for one Major Arthur McHugh, a great-great-uncle of the present McHughs, who had served with honor under Lafayette in the Revolution. The major had left behind him the reputation of great personal bravery, a portrait which showed him as extremely handsome, and the fame of having been a great lady-killer and something of a rake withal; while he had taken out of the world with him, or at least had not left behind, the secret of what he had done with the famous McHugh diamonds. Major McHugh was his father's eldest son, and in the family the law of primogeniture was in his day pretty strictly observed, so that to him descended the estate. A disappointment in love resulted in his refusing to marry, although urged thereto by his family and much reasoned with by disinterested mothers with marriageable daughters. He bequeathed the estate to the eldest son of his younger brother, who had been named for him, and this Arthur McHugh was the grandfather of the present lieutenant.

With the estate went the famous McHugh diamonds, at that time the finest in America. The "McHugh star," a huge stone of rose cut, had once been the eye of an idol in the temple of Majarah, whence it had been stolen by the sacrilegious Rajah of Zinyt, from whose possession it passed into the hands of a Colonel McHugh at the siege of Zinyt in 1707. There was an effort made, about the middle of the eighteenth century, to add this beautiful gem to the crown jewels of France, but the McHugh then at the head of the family, the father of Major McHugh, declared that he would sooner part with wife and children than with the "McHugh star," an unchristian sentiment, which speaks better for his appreciation of jewels than for his family affection.

When Major McHugh departed from this life, in 1787, the McHugh diamonds were naturally sought for by his heir, but were nowhere to be found. None of the family knew where they were usually kept—a circumstance which was really less singular than it might at first appear, since the major was never communicative, and in those days concealment was more relied upon for the safety of small valuables than the strength which the modern safe, with its misleading name, is supposed to supply. The last that was known of the gems was their being worn at a ball in 1785 by the sister-in-law of the owner, to whom they had been loaned for the occasion. Here they had attracted the greatest attention and admiration, but on their return to Major McHugh they seemed to vanish forever. Search had of course been made, and one generation after another, hearing the traditions, and believing in its own cleverness, had renewed the endeavor, but thus far the mystery had remained unsolved.

III

It was when the girls were brushing out their hair together in that hour before retiring which is traditionally sacred to feminine confidences, that Irene asked rather abruptly:—

"Well, Fanny, what is it that you want of me?"

"Want?" replied her friend, who could not possibly help being femininely evasive. "I want to see you, of course."

"Yes," the guest returned, smiling; "and that is the reason you gave me this room, which I never had before."

The hostess blushed. "It is the handsomest room in the house," she said defensively.

"And one shares it," Irene added, "with the ghost of the gallant major."

"But you know," protested Fanny, "that you do not mind ghosts in the least."

"Not so very much now that I am used to them. They are poor creatures; and it seems to me that they get feebler the more people refuse to believe in them."

"Oh, you don't suppose," cried Fanny, in the greatest anxiety, "that the major's ghost has faded away, do you? Nobody has slept here for years, so that nobody has seen it for ever so long."

"And you want me to assure it that you think it eminently respectable to have a wraith in the family, so you hope it will persevere in haunting Oldtower?"

"Oh, it isn't that at all," Fanny said, lowering her voice. "I suppose Arthur would be furious if he knew it, or that I even mentioned it, but I am sure it is more for his sake than for my own. Don't you think that it is?"

"You are simply too provoking for anything," Irene responded. "I am sure I never saw a ghost that talked so unintelligibly as you do. What in the world do you mean?"

"Why, only the other day Arthur said in joke that if somebody could only make the major's—" she looked around to indicate the word which she evidently did not care to pronounce in that chamber, and Irene nodded to signify that she understood—"if only somebody could make it tell where the McHugh diamonds are—"

"Oh, that's it, is it?" interrupted Irene. "Well, my dear, I am willing to speak to the major, if he will give me an opportunity; but it is not likely that I can do much. He will not care for what I say."

"But appeal to his family pride," Fanny said, with an earnestness that betrayed the importance of this matter to her. "Tell him how we are going to ruin for want of just the help those diamonds would give us. He ought to have some family pride left."

Miss Gaspic naturally did not wish to draw her friend into a conversation upon the financial straits of the family, and she therefore managed to turn the conversation, only repeating her promise that if the wraith of the major put in an appearance, she would do whatever lay in her power to get from him the secret which he had kept for a century. It was not long before Fanny withdrew, and, taking a book, Irene sat down to read, and await her visitor.

It was just at midnight that the major's spirit made its appearance. It was a ghost of a conventional period, and it carefully observed all the old-time conditions. Irene, who had been waiting for it, raised her eyes from the book which she had been reading, and examined it carefully. The ghost had the likeness of a handsome man of rather more than middle age and of majestic presence. The figure was dressed in Continental uniform, and in its hand carried a glass apparently full of red wine. As Irene raised her eyes, the ghost bowed gravely and courteously, and then drained the cup to its depth.

"Good-evening," Miss Gaspic said politely. "Will you be seated?"

The apparition was evidently startled by this cool address, and, instead of replying, again bowed and again drained its glass, which had in some mysterious manner become refilled.

"Thank you," Irene said, in answer to his repeated salute; "please sit down. I was expecting you, and I have something to say."

The ghost of the dead-and-gone major stared more than before.

"I beg your pardon?" he responded, in a thinly interrogative tone.

"Pray be seated," Irene invited him for the third time.

The ghost wavered into an old-fashioned high-backed chair, which remained distinctly visible through his form, and for a moment or two the pair eyed each other in silence. The situation seemed somehow to be a strained one even to the ghost.

"It seems to me," Irene said, breaking the silence, "that it would be hard for you to refuse the request of a lady."

"Oh, impossible," the ghost quavered, with old-time gallantry; "especially of a lovely creature like some we could mention. Anything," he added in a slightly altered tone, as if his experiences in ghostland had taught him the need of caution—"anything in reason, of course."

Irene smiled her most persuasive smile. "Do I look like one who would ask unreasonable things?" she asked.

"I am sure that nothing which you should ask could be unreasonable," the ghost replied, with so much gallantry that Irene had for a moment a confused sense of having lost her identity, since to have a ghost complimenting her naturally gave her much the feeling of being a ghost herself.

"And certainly the McHugh diamonds can do you no good now," Miss Gaspic continued, introducing her subject with truly feminine indirectness.

"The McHugh diamonds?" echoed the ghost stammeringly, as if the shock of the surprise, under which he grew perceptibly thinner, was almost more than his incorporeal frame could endure.

"Yes," responded Irene. "Of course I have no claim on them, but the family is in severe need, and—"

"They wish to sell my diamonds!" exclaimed the wraith, starting up in wrath. "The degenerate, unworthy—"

Words seemed to fail him, and in an agitated manner he swallowed two or three glasses of wine in quick succession.

"Why, sire," Irene asked irrelevantly, "do you seem to be always drinking wine?"

"Because," he answered sadly, "I dropped dead while I was drinking the health of Lady Betty Rafferty, and since then I have to do it whenever I am in the presence of mortals."

"But can you not stop?"

"Only when your ladyship is pleased to command me," he replied, with all his old-fashioned elaborateness of courtesy.

"And as to the diamonds," Irene said, coming back to that subject with an abruptness which seemed to be most annoying to the ghost, "of what possible use can they be to you in your present condition?"

"What use?" echoed the shade of the major, with much fierceness. "They are my occupation. I am their guardian spirit."

"But," she urged, bringing to bear those powers of logic upon which she always had prided herself, "you drink the ghost of wine, don't you?"

"Certainly, madam," the spirit answered, evidently confused.

"Then why can you not be content with guarding the ghost of the McHugh diamonds, while you let the real, live Arthur McHugh have the real stones?"

"Why, that," the apparition returned, with true masculine perversity, "is different—quite different."

"How is it different?"

"Now I am the guardian of a genuine treasure. I am the most considerable personage in our whole circle."

"Your circle?" interrupted Irene.

"You would not understand," the shape said, "so I will, with your permission, omit the explanation. If I gave up the diamonds, I should be only a common drinking ghost—a thing to be gossiped about and smiled at."

"You would be held in reverence as the posthumous benefactor of your family," she urged.

"I am better pleased with things as they are. I have no great faith in the rewards of benefactors; and the people benefited would not belong to our circle, either."

"You are both selfish and cynical," Irene declared. She fell to meditating what she had better say to him, and meanwhile she noted with satisfaction that the candle was burning blue, a fact which, to her accustomed eye, indicated that the ghost was a spirit of standing most excellent in ghostly ranks.

"To suffer the disapproval of one so lovely," the remnant of the old-time gentleman rejoined, "is a misfortune so severe that I cannot forbear reminding you that you are not fully familiar with the conditions under which I exist."

In this unsatisfactory strain the conversation continued for some time longer; and when at length the ghost took its departure, and Irene retired to rest, she could not flatter herself that she had made any especial progress toward inducing the spirit to yield the secret which it had so long and so carefully guarded. The major's affections seemed to be set with deathless constancy upon the gems, and that most powerful of masculine passions, vanity, to be enlisted in their defense.

"I am afraid that it is of no use," Irene sighed to herself; "and yet, after all, he was only a man when he was

alive, and he cannot be much more than that now when
he is a ghost."

And greatly comforted by the reflection that whatever
is masculine is to be overcome by feminine guile, she
fell asleep.

IV

On the following afternoon Irene found herself rowing
on the river with the lieutenant. She had declined his invitation to come, and had immediately felt so exultant
in the strength of mind which had enabled her to with-
stand temptation that she had followed the refusal with
an acceptance.

The day was deliciously soft and balmy. A thin haze
shut off the heat of the sun, while a southerly breeze
found somewhere a spicy and refreshing odor, which
with great generosity it diffused over the water. The
river moved tranquilly, and any one capable of being
sentimental might well find it hard to resist the influ-
ences of the afternoon.

The lieutenant was as ardently in love as it is possible
for a man to be who is at once a soldier and handsome,
and indeed more than would have been expected from
a man who combined such causes of self-satisfaction.
The fact that Irene had a great deal of money, while he
had none, gave to his passion a hopelessness from his
point of view which much increased its fervor. He
gazed at his companion with his great dark eyes as she
sat in the stern, his heavy eyebrows and well-developed
mustache preventing him from looking as silly as might
otherwise have been the case. Miss Gaspic was by no
means insensible to the spell of the time and of the
companionship in which she found herself, but she was
determined above all things to be discreet.

"Arthur," she said by way of keeping the talk in safe channels and also of finding out what she wanted to know, "was search ever made for the McHugh diamonds?"

"Search!" he repeated. "Everything short of pulling the house down has been tried. Everybody in the family from the time they were lost has had a hand at it."

"I do not see—" began Irene, when he interrupted brusquely.

"No," he said; "nobody sees. The solution of the riddle is probably so simple that nobody will think of it. It will be hit upon by accident some day. But, for the sake of goodness, let us talk of something else. I always lose my temper when the McHugh diamonds are mentioned."

He relieved his impatience by a fierce spurt at the oars, which sent the boat spinning through the water; then he shook himself as if to shake off unpleasant thoughts, and once more allowed the current to take them along. Irene looked at him with wistful eyes. She would have been so glad to give him all her money if he would have it.

"You told me," she said at length, with a faint air of self-consciousness, "that you wanted to say something to me."

The young lieutenant flushed, and looked between the trunks of the old trees on the river-bank into the far distance. "I have," he responded. "It is a piece of impertinence, because I have no right to say it to you."

"You may say anything you wish to say," Irene answered, while a vague apprehension took possession of her mind at something in his tone. "Surely we have known each other long enough for that."

"Well," the other blurted out with an abruptness that showed the effort that it cost him, "you should be married, Irene."

Irene felt like bursting into tears, but with truly feminine fortitude she managed to smile instead.

"Am I getting so woefully old and faded, then, Arthur?" she asked.

His look of reproachful denial was sufficiently eloquent to need no added word. "Of course not," he said; "but you should not be going on toward the time when—"

"When I shall be," she concluded his sentence as he hesitated. "Then, Arthur, why don't you ask me to marry you?"

The blood rushed into his face and ebbed away, leaving him as pale as so sun-browned a fellow could well be. He set his teeth together over a word which was strangled in its utterance, and Irene saw with secret admiration the mighty grasp of his hands upon the oars. She could be proud of his self-control so long as she was satisfied of the intensity of his feelings, and she was almost as keenly thrilled by the adoring, appealing look in his brown eyes as she would have been by a caress.

"Because," he said, "the McHughs have never yet been set down as fortune-hunters, and I do not care to be the one to bring that reproach upon the family."

"What a vilely selfish way of looking at it!" she cried.

"Very likely it seems so to a woman."

Irene flushed in her turn, and for fully two minutes there was no sound save that of the water lapping softly against the boat. Then Miss Gaspic spoke again.

"It is possible," she said, in a tone so cold that the poor lieutenant dared not answer her, "that the fact that you are a man prevents you from understanding how a woman feels who has thrown herself at a man's head, as

I have done, and been rejected. Take me back to the shore."

And he had not a word to answer.

V

To have proposed to a man, and been refused, is not a soothing experience for any woman; and although the ground upon which Arthur had based his rejection was one which Irene had before known to be the obstacle between them, the refusal remained a stubborn fact to rankle in her mind. All the evening she nursed her wounded feelings, and by the time midnight brought her once more face to face with the ghost of the major, her temper was in a state which nothing save the desire to shield a lady could induce one to call by even so mild a word as uncertain.

The spirit appeared as usual, saluting, and tossing off bumpers from its shadowy wine-glass, and it had swallowed at least a dozen cups before Miss Gaspic condescended to indicate that she was aware of its presence.

"Why do you stand there drinking in that idiotic fashion?" she demanded, with more asperity than politeness. "Once is quite enough for that sort of thing."

"But I cannot speak until I have been spoken to," the ghost responded apologetically, "and I have to continue drinking until I have been requested to do something else."

"Drink, then, by all means," Irene replied coldly, turning to pick up a book. "I only hope that so much wine will not go to your head."

"But it is sure to," the ghost said, in piteous tones; "and in all my existence, even when I was only a man, I have never been overcome with wine in the presence of a lady."

It continued to swallow the wraith of red wine while it spoke, and Irene regarded it curiously.

"An inebriated ghost," she observed dispassionately, "is something which it is so seldom given to mortal to see that it would be the greatest of folly to neglect this opportunity of getting sight of that phenomenon."

"Please tell me to go away, or to sit down, or to do something," the quondam major pleaded.

"Then tell me where the McHugh diamonds are," she said.

A look of desperate obstinacy came into the ghost's face, through which could unpleasantly be seen the brass knobs of a tall secretary on the opposite side of the room. For some moments the pair confronted each other in silence, although the apparition continued its drinking. Irene watched the figure with unrelenting countenance, and at length made the curious discovery that it was standing upon tiptoe. In a moment more she saw that it was really rising, and that its feet from time to time left the carpet entirely. Her first thought was a fear that it was about to float away and escape, but upon looking closer she came to the conclusion that it was endeavoring to resist the tendency to rise into the air. Watching more sharply, she perceived that while with its right hand it raised its inexhaustible wine-cup, with its left it clung to the back of a chair in an evident endeavor to keep itself down.

"You seem to be standing on tiptoe," she observed. "Were you looking for anything?"

"No," the wraith responded, in evident confusion; "that is merely the levitation consequent upon this constant imbibing."

Irene laughed contemptuously. "Do you mean," she demanded unfeelingly, "that the sign of intoxication in a ghost is a tendency to rise into the air?"

"It is considered more polite in our circle to use the

45

term employed by the occultists," the apparition answered somewhat sulkily. "We speak of it as 'levitation.'"

"But I do not belong to your circle," Irene returned cheerfully, "and I am not in sympathy with the occultists. Does it not occur to you," she went on, "that it is worth while to take into consideration the fact that in these progressive times you do not occupy the same place in popular or even in scientific estimation which was yours formerly? You are now merely an hallucination, you know, and there is no reason that I should regard you with anything but contempt, as a mere symptom of indigestion or of mental fatigue."

"But you can see that I am not an hallucination, can you not?" quavered the poor ghost of the major, evidently becoming dreadfully discouraged.

"Oh, that is simply a delusion of the senses," Irene made answer in a matter-of-fact way, which, even while she spoke, she felt to be basely cruel. "Any physician would tell me so, and would write out a prescription for me to prevent my seeing you again."

"But he couldn't" the ghost said, with pathetic feebleness.

"You do not know the physicians of today," she replied, with a smile. "But to drop that, what I wished to say was this: does it not seem to you that this is a good opportunity to prove your reality by showing me the hiding-place of the diamonds? I give you my word that I will report the case to the Psychical Research Society, and you will then go on record and have a permanent reputation which the incredulity of the age cannot destroy."

The ghost was by this time in a state of intoxication which evidently made it able only with the utmost difficulty to keep from sailing to the ceiling. It clung to the back of a chair with a desperate clutch, while its feet paddled hopelessly and helplessly in the air, in vain attempts once more to get into touch with the floor.

"But the Psychical Research Society is not recognized in my circle," it still objected.

"Very well," Irene exclaimed in exasperation; "do as you like! But what will be the effect upon your reputation if you go floating helplessly back to your circle in your present condition? Is levitation in the presence of ladies considered respectable in this society of whose opinion you think so much?"

"Oh, to think of it!" the spirit of the bygone major wailed with a sudden shrillness of woe which made even Miss Gaspic's blood run cold. "Oh, the disgrace of it! I will do anything you ask."

Irene sprang to her feet in sudden excitement.

"Will you show me—" she began; but the wavering voice of the ghost interrupted her.

"You must lead me," it said. "Give me your hand. I shall float up to the ceiling if I let go my hold upon this chair."

"Your hand—that is, I—I don't like the feeling of ghosts," Irene replied. "Here, take hold of this."

She picked up a pearl paper-knife and extended it toward the spirit. The ghost grasped it, and in this manner was led down the chamber, floating and struggling upward like a bird. Irene was surprised at the amount of force with which it pulled at the paper-knife, but she reflected that it had really swallowed an enormous quantity of its ghostly stimulant. She followed the directions of the waving hand that held the wine-glass, and in this way they came to a corner of the room where the spirit made signs that it wished to get nearer the floor. Irene pulled the figure downward, until it crouched in the corner. It laid one transparent hand upon a certain panel in the wainscoting.

"Search here," it said.

In the excitement of the moment Irene relaxed her hold upon the paper-knife. Instantly the ghost floated upward like a balloon released from its moorings, while the paper-knife dropped through its incorporeal form to the floor.

"Good-by," Irene cried after it. "Thank you so much!"

And like a blurred and dissolving cloud above her head the intoxicated ghost faded into nothingness.

VI

It was hardly to be expected that Irene, flushed with the proud delight of having triumphed over the obstinate ghost of the major, could keep her discovery to herself for so long a time as until daylight. It was already near one in the morning, but on going to her window, and looking across to the wing of the house where the lieutenant's rooms were, she saw that his light was still burning. With a secret feeling that he was probably reflecting upon the events of the afternoon, Irene sped along the passage to the door of Fanny's chamber, whom she awakened, and dispatched to bring Arthur.

Fanny's characteristically feminine manner of calling her brother was to dash into his room, crying:—

"Oh, Arthur, Irene has found the McHugh diamonds!"

She was too incoherent to reply to his questions, so that there was manifestly nothing for him to do but to follow to the place where Irene was awaiting them. There the young couple were deserted by Fanny, who impulsively ran on before to the haunted chamber, leaving them to follow. As they walked along the corridor, the lieutenant, who perhaps felt that it was well not to provoke a discussion which might call up too vividly in

Irene's mind the humiliation of the afternoon, clasped her quite without warning, and drew her to his side.

"Now I can ask you to marry me," he said; "and I love you, Irene, with my whole heart."

Her first movement was an instinctive struggle to free herself; but the persuasion of his embrace was too sweet to be resisted, and she only protested by saying, "Your love seems to depend very much upon those detestable old diamonds."

"Of course," he answered. "Without them I am too poor to have any right to think of you."

"Oh," she cried out in sudden terror, "suppose that they are not there!"

The young man loosened his embrace in astonishment.

"Not there!" he repeated. "Fanny said that you had found them."

"Not yet; only the ghost—"

"The ghost!" he echoed, in tones of mingled disappointment and chagrin. "Is that all there is to it?"

Irene felt that her golden love-dream was rudely shattered. She was aware that the lieutenant did not even believe in the existence of the wraith of the major, and although she had been conversing with the spirit for so long a time that very night, so great was the influence of her lover over her mind that she began at this moment to doubt the reality of the apparition herself.

With pale face and sinking heart she led the way into her chamber, and to the corner where the paper-knife yet lay upon the floor in testimony of the actuality of her interview with the wraith. Under her directions the panel was removed from the wainscot, a labor which was not effected without a good deal of difficulty. Arthur sneered at the whole thing, but he yet was good-natured enough to do what the girls asked of him.

Only the dust of centuries rewarded their search.

When it was fully established that there were no jewel-cases there, poor Irene broke down entirely, and burst into convulsive weeping.

"There, there," Arthur said soothingly. "Don't feel like that. We've got on without the diamonds thus far, and we can still."

"It isn't the diamonds that I'm crying for," sobbed Irene, with all the naïveté of a child that has lost its pet toy. "It's you!"

There was no withstanding this appeal. Arthur took her into his arms and comforted her, while Fanny discreetly looked the other way; and so the engagement was allowed to stand, although the McHugh diamonds had not been found.

VII

But the next night Irene faced the ghost with an expression of contempt that might have withered the spirit of Hamlet's sire.

"So you think it proper to deceive a lady?" she inquired scornfully. "Is that the way in which the gentlemen of the 'old school,' of which we hear so much, behaved?"

"Why, you should reflect," the wraith responded waveringly, "that you had made me intoxicated." And, indeed, the poor spirit still showed the effects of its debauch.

"You cannot have been very thoroughly intoxicated," Irene returned, "or you would not have been able to deceive me."

"But you see," it answered, "that I drank only the ghost of wine, so that I really had only the ghost of inebriation."

"But being a ghost yourself," was her reply, "that should have been enough to intoxicate you completely."

"I never argue with a lady," said the ghost loftily, the subject evidently being too complicated for it to follow further. "At least I managed to put you as far as possible on the wrong scent."

As it spoke, it gave the least possible turn of its eye toward the corner of the room diagonally opposite to that where it had disappeared on the previous night.

"Ah!" cried Irene, with sudden illumination.

She sprang up, and began to move from its place in the corner an old secretary which stood there. The thing was very heavy, but she did not call for help. She strained and tugged, the ghost showing evident signs of perturbation, until she had thrust the secretary aside, and then with her lamp beside her she sat down upon the floor and began to examine the wainscoting.

"Come away, please," the ghost said piteously. "I hate to see you there on the floor. Come and sit by the fire."

"Thank you," she returned. "I am very comfortable where I am."

She felt of the panels, she poked and pried, and for more than an hour she worked, while the ghost stood over her, begging that she go away. It was just as she was on the point of giving up that her fingers, rubbing up and down, started a morsel of dust from a tiny hold in the edge of a panel. She seized a hairpin from amid her locks, and thrust the point into the little opening. The panel started, moved slowly on a concealed hinge, and opened enough for her to insert her fingers and to push it back. A sort of closet lay revealed, and in it was a pile of cases, dusty, moth-eaten, and time-stained. She seized the first that came to hand, and opened it. There upon its bed of faded velvet blazed the "McHugh star," superb in its beauty and a fortune in itself.

51

"Oh, my diamonds!" shrilled the ghost of Major McHugh. "Oh, what will our circle say!"

"They will have the right to say that you were rude to a lady," Irene answered, with gratuitous severity. "You have wasted your opportunity of being put on record."

"Now I am only a drinking ghost!" the wraith wailed, and faded away upon the air.

Thus it came about that on her wedding-day Irene wore the "McHugh star;" and yet, such is human perversity that she has not only been convinced by her husband that ghosts do not exist, but she has lost completely the power of seeing them, although that singular and valuable gift had come to her, as has been said, by inheritance from a great-aunt on her mother's side of the family.

THE GOLDEN RAT

Alexander Harvey

What secret of her troubled soul could the youthful and lovely wife of old Gerald Lancaster be concealing now from me? She was decidedly the most baffling of all my patients. I was comparatively young, as men in the professions reckon age, yet I had devoted eleven arduous years to the practice of that department of psychology which goes by the name of psycho-analysis. It seemed obvious, from the very first appearance of the lady in my consultation room, that she suffered from the shock of an underlying emotional disturbance. Mrs. Lancaster, that is to say, had passed through a painful experience. She had striven to banish it from her consciousness.

Now what had been the emotional disturbance in her case? I could but conjecture vaguely. Her experience, whatever it had been, was not extinguished. It remained latent in her sub-consciousness, buried below the level of her waking mentality. The case of Mrs. Lancaster was, to use the technical phraseology one of repression, the experience or emotion which she strove to put out of her mind and her life being what we psychologists call a "complex."

As I concentrated my gaze upon the large but troubled eyes of Mrs. Lancaster, it dawned upon me that the "complex"—the idea or sorrow she strove to annihilate—was emotional, sentimental. Had she formed some unhappy attachment which the fiercest efforts of her will failed to subdue? I made the suggestion which seemed to me the best possible under the circumstances.

"I shall have to hypnotize you."

Speaking in the fluted accents which made her voice harmonize so perfectly with the sweetness of her face, Mrs. Lancaster objected to the very idea. She declined to be hypnotized because she feared the process might undermine the strength of her will. It was not difficult to reassure her on this point. To my surprise, however, I found my patient absolutely unhypnotizable. There remained only the alternative of imploring her to tell me frankly all that was in her mind, all that might be below the level of her consciousness, all that she would hide even from herself.

"I fear," I remarked, as considerately as I could—"I fear you are concealing something from me—something of which you do not perhaps realize the importance or even the nature."

She searched her memory in vain. I had, on the occasion of our last interview in my study, forborne to press her. It was my hope that in the course of a subsequent consultation I should elicit the mysterious cause of her nervous state.

How well I remember that summer afternoon! The wife of old Lancaster had taken her departure, and I stood absorbed in baffling reflections with reference to this most mysterious patient. Slowly, at last, I opened the door that afforded access to the garden stretching from my study window quite to the stables. The garden, like the stables themselves, was a luxury, a whim of mine. The value of improved real estate in my native city made the taxes upon my cultivated acres anything but a trifle. I might have kept a motor car, but my love of horseflesh made it impossible to give up the stables for a garage.

"More rats, doctor."

It was Boggs, the grim coachman. I found him rubbing down the most spirited of the steeds behind which it pleased me to spin through the streets of the city. Boggs indicated a pail near one of the stalls.

I gazed vacantly at the nestful of tiny young rats. My mind was still absorbed by the repressed "complex" of the puzzling Mrs. Lancaster. I still stared at the seven blind, feeble creatures, too young for even a growth of hair to be manifest upon their hides. Boggs had stepped over to my side by this time. He clutched the nozzle of a streaming line of hose.

"I'll drown 'em, drat 'em!"

He would have flooded the wriggling nestful in a trice had I not stayed his hand.

"That little fellow there," I remarked—"he looks different—lighter than the others."

Boggs peered down into the bottom of the pail.

"Yes, doctor," he conceded, his voice thick with the disgust and annoyance the sight of rats in the stables invariably caused him. "One there is yellow-like."

To the amazement of the honest Boggs, I plunged my hand among the young rats and picked up the specimen that had caught my eye. There he lay now, in the palm of my hand, blind, weak, helpless. The hairs upon his odd little frame were sparse. They were sufficiently thick, none the less, to impart an aspect of fluffy gold to his coat. I was half inclined to drop him to his doom among his brothers when his tiny tail waved vaguely. It was covered nearly to the tip with a growth of down that made it look like a golden wand. Before Boggs had closed his mouth from sheer wonder at my behavior, I had slipped the baby rat into a pocket of my coat.

Slowly I retraced my steps across the grass from the stables to the study door. I was in some perplexity. Should I risk an experiment with the tiny thing breathing still in my pocket? The query vexed me as I paced from the desk in my little study to the door of the laboratory beyond. In this laboratory were stored the test tubes, the culture mediums, the beef broth and the apparatus for clarifying and sterilizing through the medium of which I enlarged the range of my biological knowledge by artificial cultivation of bacteria. Here, too, were the cages in which, at one time, I had bred three generations of white mice. The creatures were all dead long since. I was quite an adept, however, in the care of these rodents. Many a specimen had been inoculated in this laboratory with "cultures" of my own.

Lifting the little rat from my pocket, I laid him, seemingly more dead than alive, in one of my small cages. A spirit lamp had next to be set aflame. With its aid I soon heated enough milk to fill a small bottle, from the corked neck of which protruded a tiny quill. The little rat absorbed the first meal I gave him greedily enough. I had the satisfaction of seeing him curled snugly in sleep upon a litter of scrapped rags before the milk was half consumed.

Many days had not elapsed before I saw the hair upon his coat grow sleek and plentiful. To my surprise, the yellowish tint which had first attracted my attention to the young rat deepened into one of fine gold before I possessed him a week. In a fortnight he was strong enough to climb the side of the box which was his home in my laboratory. He ran about the floor so recklessly that I was forced to keep a careful lookout for stray cats and dogs. My original fear that he would prefer the freedom of the open air or of the cellarage to my laboratory proved groundless. He seemed to be destitute of the quality of timidity. Never in my experience of pets had I acquired one so recklessly tame. It was a source of perennial delight to him to spring from my shoe to the hem of my trousers and climb up to my shoulder. There he remained perched contentedly while I read or wrote or even walked about. As day succeeded day, the exquisite golden color of his coat grew richer. I discovered his tastes in edibles, especially for roasted chestnuts, and gratified it to the full. He seemed to tire of bread and milk as he grew fatter and more golden of hue. I fed him upon cake and nuts. His place of refuge, when pressed for one, was the pocket of my coat. Again and again have I felt him stirring about there while I received a patient in my study. When we were left at last alone, he would peep forth prettily and give a little shriek of delight while returning to my shoulder.

Never was quadruped more careful of its personal appearance. The golden rat balanced itself on its hind legs to lick its belly clean, and it had a trick of wiping itself all over with its forepaws. One of these paws would be passed over the head and the ears and licked into an immaculate cleanliness at each wipe. Philander, for that was the name I bestowed upon the golden rat, was a dazzling spectacle when the light from my study lamp fell upon him. He slept for an hour at a time on the desk before which I sat to read, seeming motionless, a gleaming ornament that might have come in perfect beauty from the cunning of the hand of Benvenuto Cellini.

Philander was washing his golden coat as he sat on my shoulder one morning, when we were interrupted by the unexpected arrival of a patient. The rat—he was a good-sized animal now—took refuge in my pocket the instant old Pawkins was announced. Pawkins, I should explain, was one of the prominent bankers of the city, who had long been under my care because of his neurasthenia. It had not been easy for me in the beginning to trace the source of his disorder. It seemed due primarily to an idea implanted in his mind by the physician who first treated his symptoms. Pawkins had been told that he was threatened with Bright's disease. He had seized this diagnosis eagerly. His ailment was, on its physical side, solely due to a false suggestion. Unfortunately, however, I found it no easy matter to win my way to his confidence. There was in his mind, latent and unconquerable, a suppressed "complex," an idea he would not avow, a thought that held him prisoner. No effort of mine could bring it to the surface. In accordance with my practice, I did not force the revelation I sought from old Pawkins. I was content to bide my time, as I was biding my time with the wife of Lancaster.

The elderly financier had barely seated himself in a chair facing me when I got a sudden fright. It seemed as if he had brought a dog with him. I thought of Philander in my pocket and had difficulty in suppressing an impulse of alarm. A closer inspection of the crouching figure at the feet of old Pawkins sufficed to correct my blunder. It was no dog that sat so near him. It was rather a shadowy outline than a reality, a suggestion of a shape. As I gazed the thing seemed to be a wolf—or shall I say the wraith of a wolf? A minute or two elapsed before I could withdraw my gaze from what I felt now must be a spectre. I had seen what was too evidently a ghost, for when I dropped my eyes once more to the floor the thing had disappeared.

It was easy enough to get rid of old Pawkins after a few perfunctory questions. When he had taken his departure, I gave myself up to a profound reverie. Philander had emerged from his retreat and was gorging himself on the floor with roasted chestnuts. It was borne in upon me at this moment, for the first time, that some connection must exist between the golden rat and a series of emotional and physical experiences and sensations in myself. I asked myself if the golden rat had not communicated to me the symptoms of that fevered state in which I now so often found myself. The state was one of exhilaration—like the first effects of some delightful stimulant. It was an exhilaration which wore away. It left, unlike the thrills that go with opium, no baneful consequences. It brought me a singular capacity to verify with my own eye—at intervals—the fact that practically all sources of illumination emit an ultraviolet light playing no part in ordinary vision. This is the result of the circumstance that the eye is sensitive only to a small proportion of the radiation reaching it. There were times, however, when my eyes became more than ever camera-like, detecting and measuring the intensity of what physicists call the infrared rays. I could see at such times by the aid of a light which physicists have pronounced invisible or at least discernible only through photography.

It occurred to me, after the departure of old Pawkins, that the wolf I had seen at his feet was an optical eccentricity in me. I recalled just then a fit of trembling in Philander while he lay concealed in my pocket. I recalled, too, the peculiarities of his conduct when certain other patients were in my study. The golden rat was subject to an inexplicable panic whenever the wife of a certain clergyman poured the tale of her neurosis into my ear. Philander took refuge under a bookcase or in the remotest recesses of a drawer in my desk. My eye chanced to light upon his frolicking form as I pondered these things. He held a walnut in his forepaws and, perched upon his hind limbs like an educated poodle, was devouring the morsel greedily. I waited until he had satisfied his appetite and then called him by his name. In a trice he was upon my shoulder.

The exigencies of a laboratory experiment that day required the use of a pair of black silk gloves. These were in my lap. The rat was creeping around my neck as I drew one of these gloves over my left hand, fitting it snugly and carefully from force of habit, although my mind was engaged solely with the mystery of the Pawkins wolf. On a sudden I saw a minute speck moving against the blackness of the glove. It was a mere mite of a speck, but it shone in golden luster as it flitted and fluttered.

The darting and dancing mite in the palm of my gloved hand was a flea.

A flood of light was let into every nook and cranny of my mind the moment I had caught the golden insect on the tip of my finger with the aid of a dab of vaseline. Philander, then, was infested with fleas. They were like himself in their peculiarly golden aspect. I brought the rat from his place of rest on my shoulder down to my knee. The critical inspection of his fur to which I abandoned myself—not neglecting a microscope in the process—revealed a quantity of golden fleas. I was unable to identify the species. It is true that the varieties of flea already classified are infinite. I had studied a few in my student days. Here was a species as new as it was strange. There could be no doubt that the fleas on Philander had been the agents of the spread of some infection to me. My symptoms of late had been very puzzling.

I was quite certain that Philander could not have imparted to me the bacillus of any infection so dire as plague. That dread disease appears only in fleas which have bitten affected rats or persons at least twelve hours prior to death. The organism causing the disease itself must exist for a certain interval in the body of Philander, there to undergo a definite alteration, before it could induce an infection in me by transmission through the flea. And there was no known case of plague affecting a human being sufficiently near to involve Philander in the slightest suspicion.

The dilemma of my situation seemed greater on the following morning. I found my fever slightly higher, although the exhilaration was quite pleasant. I observed an accentuation of the eccentricity of my vision. I detected ultra-violet light without the aid of an instrument. There was one close friend to whom I could turn in this crisis. Having ascertained over the telephone that Thorburn, the renowned specialist, who had been my classmate at the medical school, could receive me at once, I hastened to his office.

My brilliant friend, whose researches in microbiology fill the world with his fame, had a touch or two of gray at the temples, I noticed. He received me most effusively, for we had not met in a long time. My eye was held for a minute, as we shook hands, by the large stork standing gravely at Thorburn's side.

"Are you fond of storks?"

I asked the question smilingly. He looked at me in some surprise.

"Not particularly," he replied. "Why?"

It flashed through my mind at once that this bird by Thorburn's side was no more real than the wolf at Pawkins' feet.

"Why?" I repeated, a flash of inspiration rescuing me from the dilemma. "You have been married six years and you have no children."

His face clouded at once.

"You are a great psychologist," I heard him murmur, as if he were talking to himself. "You have guessed the

61

longing that fills my heart, the preoccupation of my life."

I saw now what the stork meant. It was the symbol of the desire in my friend's heart, the thought that would not leave him, the longing he had put out of his mind. His wish for a child to bless his union with Florella had been put from the upper level of his consciousness into that lower level of forgetfulness where his "repressed complex" lay buried. All men living, I knew, bore in their minds the wishes, the aspirations, they had buried in the well of the subconsciousness. Not until this moment did I suspect that the longing buried in the mind, the fond wish one dare not avow but over which one gloated inwardly, was a wraith, a ghost. Thorburn's buried wish was haunting him. The stork at his side was its ghost.

Not a word of all this escaped me; no hint of the presence of the grave bird passed my lips. I laid my case before him to the extent of avowing my fear of some infection. He examined me from head to foot. He made every laboratory test possible in the circumstances. As he came and went, now peering into my eyes, again holding a tube aloft in the bright electric light of his laboratory, I saw the stork follow him, sit at his feet, flap noiseless wings or prepare for some wild flight that was never even attempted.

"There is no organic disorder," was Thorburn's report at last. "I see no evidence yet of the presence of any infection. I can let you know definitely in a week."

The stork, invisible to Thorburn, eyed me gravely as I took my leave. In much perplexity I walked slowly to my home, letting myself in with my own key and repairing to my study with a profound problem on my mind. The first thing was to find Philander. He had a trick of fashioning a nest for himself out of old newspapers under a corner of my desk. I called him by name.

There was no response. At first I suspected him of hiding from me by design, a thing he was very prone to when he feared being shut up in his cage for the night. He had a great affection for the chimney. The soot in that retreat begrimed his coat most sadly, although he never failed to wash himself clean the moment he emerged. There had been no fire in my study since the spring. I thrust my head into the empty grate and called his name loudly. There was again no response.

I was not in any great alarm. He had a way of disappearing now and then, sometimes for as long as twenty-four hours. My one dread was that a stray cat or dog might pounce upon my pet. There was now nothing for it but to compose myself in my easy chair and ponder the events of this day.

My eye wandered vacantly over the papers and test tubes forming a litter in front of me until a gleam of something like light, a flash like the twinkle of a distant star, enchained my glance. The shimmer and slash were a series of stains upon a handkerchief. I picked up the silken article in some bewilderment at first. It looked like some fantastic flag with suns in gold designed upon its center. My own initials worked in a corner of the piece of silk brought back to my recollection a slight bleeding of the nose which had troubled me that morning. I had applied this silk handkerchief to my face. The slight hemorrhage ceased. I had given the matter no further thought. Now I saw spots of shining gold where in the morning my blood had stained this piece of silk a bright red.

In my bewilderment I took the handkerchief over to the window. There could be no doubt now of the brightness of the gold. Never in my experience had I heard of man or woman who bled gold. I resolved to despatch the handkerchief to Thorburn for an immediate analysis. The ringing of the bell, a voice at the door and the entrance of a visitor postponed the execution of this purpose.

"And how is our rising young psychoanalyst?" cried a cheery voice, as a burly form broke rather than appeared through the door. "Upon my word, that last talk of yours upon the mental mechanism of the banished idea has made you famous."

My visitor carried with him, I saw now, a late number of the official organ of a psychological society. One of my studies was given a very prominent place in the periodical. I glanced at the printed page and then rose to greet old Graham. I dearly loved this man, for he had been one of my most honored preceptors in my student days.

"My dear Graham!" I cried.

A silvery dove fluttered about his head, but I was accustomed by this time to my capacity for this species of visualization and I betrayed by neither word nor glance the effect of the sight upon me. The dove, I could see, corresponded to the system of ideas making up the "complex" of this good and generous man. What a contract to the predatory old Pawkins, whose repressed ideas emerged in spite of himself under the guise of a wolf—at least to my vision! It has been well said that in the psychical sphere complexes have an action resembling that of energy in the physical sphere. A system of ideas may lie latent in a man's mind for a long time, becoming active only when stimulated. This explained, no doubt, why the dove hovering over old Doctor Graham flitted out of sight now and then.

"My boy," said the old man, looking somewhat anxiously about him before he sank into the chair I brought, "are we alone?"

I nodded. There was an anxiety on his mind which became more manifest as he proceeded:

"You may have heard that one or two well-defined

cases of plague came recently to the notice of the board."

I recalled such a report. I had first heard of the matter at a gathering of physicians some time before. Graham, who was in the service of the Board of Health, had taken the matter seriously at the time, but the affair had dropped out of my thoughts long since. The old man leaned forward to impress me with what he had now to say:

"The cases have been increasing. We have made up our minds to make war on the rats."

"The rats!"

I spoke in a tone of some consternation. The words brought the missing Philander back to my memory.

"The rats," repeated Graham solemnly. "We have actually discovered the bacillus in the bodies of no less than three rats."

"Were they rats caught in the city?"

"In this very neighborhood. We have been quietly trapping here and there. We don't want to start a plague panic until we are sure of our facts."

I watched the dove flitting above his head and I thought of Philander. Had they trapped the golden rat? I had to steady my voice with an effort before I could put my question:

"These rats—they are the ordinary gray variety?"

The elderly physician looked troubled.

"Yes—and no," said he slowly. "Our traps have contained gray rats as a rule. But in two instances we have captured a very peculiar variety of the animal—gray rats with a spot of gold on the breast."

He drew from his pocket as he spoke a small leather casket. It opened at the touch of a spring. I saw the stuffed skin of a gray rat, splashed in the spot indicated with gleaming gold.

"This rat," explained old Graham, lifting the stuffed

65

object up for my inspection, "was trapped in the house next door. It is one of six marked in this very extraordinary manner—a species never seen before by any authority I have consulted."

I took the stuffed rat from the grasp of my elderly friend and examined its aspect critically. Those who have never studied at first hand the habits of a rodent of such sinister fame can form no idea of the natural cleanliness of the little animal. Apart from the tendency of the flea to infest the rat, it is one of the daintiest of quadrupeds, not, indeed, without a beauty of its own. The spot of gold between the forepaws of this specimen set off its gray coat effectively.

"Although we have trapped rats all over the city," proceeded old Graham earnestly, "they are all of the usual gray type except those few caught next door. I have just been setting traps in your cellar."

The thought of Philander made my blood run cold at these words. I gazed in blank dismay at the physician. What had become of the golden rat?

"Have you"—I faltered before I could speak the question completely—"caught anything here?"

"My dear lad, the traps have just been set—two of them. I can let you know the result in a few days."

"You spoke just now," I resumed, in as natural a voice as I could command, "of having isolated the bacillus in the blood of some of your rats. How about these?"

Graham took the stuffed rat from me and looked it over.

"We have isolated a most curious organism in the blood stream of this little creature," he observed. "A golden microbe."

"What disease does it cause?"

I tried again to speak naturally, but I remembered the golden blood I had shed and felt faint. What if I had acquired a new and strange leprosy from the bite of the golden fleas of Philander!

"Strange as it must seem," I now heard Graham aver, "the microbe—it is really a bacillus with its nucleus and protoplasm—gives rise to no discoverable disease in the rat infected by it. Perhaps it is responsible for the gold spot."

He touched the flaming breast of the stuffed creature.

"The remarkable thing," the old doctor added, "is the golden element in the rod-like process of these organisms. One might almost say the blood of this rat was golden."

My mind reverted to the analysis of my own blood cells which Thorburn was at that moment engaged upon.

"You don't mean to say," I rejoined, smiling, "that you have discovered a form of bacteria that is beneficial to the invaded organism?"

"I'll know more about that when I have trapped more of these rats," the old man told me. "I expect to get some here by the end of the week."

The moment he had taken his leave, which he did almost immediately, the dove fluttering out with him, I rang up Thorburn.

"Come over at once, if you can," he said at the other end of the wire. "I have news for you."

I put on my hat and paced the streets hurriedly. I caught sight of a policeman at the corner taking a prisoner to the lockup. The man in the toils of the law was obviously a beggar. At his heels trotted a snow-white lamb. The policeman was followed by a hawk. I turned and gazed after the pair until both had disappeared around a corner. Was I doomed to see at the heels of every fellow creature the symbol of his suppressed idea, the ghost of his complex? I fairly raced to Thorburn's door.

"There is something very remarkable here," was his

first utterance, as he led the way to his laboratory. "What do you make of that?"

He held up a glass slide of the sort used in experimental biology. It was stained with a golden spot.

"Your blood," said he. "It has yielded a pure gold bacterium of the strangest character. Your blood is like the stream in which King Midas bathed—filled with golden sands."

He had scarcely said the words when a movement of flapping wings behind him drew my eyes to the stork. It stood for a moment erect and then retreated to the remotest corner of the laboratory, where it regarded both of us with all its characteristic solemnity. Thorburn was unaware of the ghostly presence. He sat me down in a great chair and questioned me most minutely regarding my symptoms.

"You must have contracted a disease of some sort," was his final verdict.

"Fatal?"

"I am using the word in a technical sense," he laughed, seeing my sober visage. "Disease is, in one aspect, the invasion of one organism by another. Your organism has been invaded by a new and strange bacterium, all gold. You say it does not debilitate you?"

"I never felt better in my life."

I glanced unshrinkingly into his puzzled face. I had carefully concealed from him the fact that I had acquired the novel faculty of beholding the repressed complexes of my fellow creatures.

"Your disease," he went on, "whatever it may be, is the effect of the interaction of two different organisms, just as plague is such an effect, or malaria."

"A new idea?"

"Not at all," retorted Thorburn. "It is not generally disseminated, of course, yet. Since disease is but the effect of one organism upon another, there is necessarily such a thing as an evolution in disease. A disease that has long been among men is a very different thing from the same disease when it first appeared on earth. The lizard is but the survivor of a far more powerful and far more intelligent creature."

I had caught the idea in his mind. The sudden appearance of a new organism is a possible thing, as the mutation theory of evolution has convinced the world. May not a totally new disease make its appearance among men, thanks to the emergence of a fresh form among the bacteria? Has not Burbank evolved new forms of vegetable life by a seeming miracle of metamorphosis? But this was by no means all that Thorburn meant. May it not be that the bacteria which cause disease are prejudicial only because they represent types of degeneracy? They have been corrupted, that is to say, by passing in and out of the blood streams of a fallen human race. It is we who have poisoned the bacteria, not the bacteria which have poisoned us. In that event, science is on the wrong track. We must purify ourselves, in order that the microbe may regain its pristine purity and become the blessing it may have been to our prehistoric ancestors.

I remained in a profound reverie long after Thorburn had finished his elucidation. If what he told me was true, I had acquired an infection, but it was a benevolent process, a source of strength. The flea had transferred to me from the body of Philander an organism that endowed me with a more wonderful power than had been possessed before by any mortal man.

"By the way," remarked Thorburn, suddenly changing the subject, "shall you be at Mrs. Lancaster's dance to-morrow night?"

I started at mention of that name. It had been weeks since I had given a thought to my patient. I replied vaguely that I expected to dine at her house. My mind was running on Philander once more, and I bade him adieu with some abruptness.

There was not the least trace of the presence of the golden rat when I arrived breathless once more in my study. I called him by name more than once. In vain. I thought of the trap set by old Graham. Before visiting the cellars I resolved to peer up the fire-place.

"Philander!" I called. "Philander!" There was a faint sound up the chimney. In a trice I had thrust my arm up the sooty embrasure. Philander descended, clinging to the sleeve of my coat. What a begrimed and blackened aspect his body now wore! I set him upon my desk, where he fell to an assiduous licking and washing of his fur. I had the satisfaction of seeing him restored to his original color before he had completed his toilet. Then he frisked his way to my shoulder, upon which he perched with all his familiar sauciness.

It was vitally important to keep Philander out of reach of the trap set for him. I might have ordered the stableman to remove the horrid instrument, to be sure. Yet that might inspire too much wonder in the mind of old Graham. On the other hand, I must not let the golden rat out of my sight. He spent the night securely locked in his cage. He was not released during the entire next day. His squeaks of protest were incessant. I would have no mercy on him.

After some reflection, I resolved to attend the dinner and dance at the house of Mrs. Lancaster. It seemed the surest method of providing for the safety of Philander. It would be no difficult thing to take him with me, concealed in the pocket of my coat. The golden rat was always shy when strangers were about. I knew that nothing could lure him from the refuge my clothes afforded him if there seemed the least prospect that he might be handled by an unfamiliar acquaintance.

The hour appointed for the dinner at the house of

Mrs. Lancaster was already chiming when I entered the dining-room. The guests were barely a dozen. I was already familiar with their faces. Philander was snugly ensconced in a breast pocket of my dress coat. He was fast asleep.

"What a stranger you are, doctor!"

The words were uttered by my fair hostess. I had never seen a more pensive melancholy upon her exquisite features. She sat at some distance from me at the foot of the table. I made my very best bow and smiled before I sat down to the oysters.

"Ha!" exclaimed Thorburn, who chanced to be seated directly opposite me. "You are looking very well—still."

There was a meaning smile upon his kindly features, and I was at no loss to interpret it. The silent stork at his side peered myopically into my face and flapped a pair of wings. I saw the hideous wolf peering greedily from beneath the chair of old Pawkins, who absorbed champagne moodily. Old Lancaster had a fierce ferret on his shoulder, a circumstance to which I was inclined to attribute the restlessness of Philander, who stirred now and then in his sleep. The most interesting object at the dinner table to me was a hyena, which chafed and fretted at the back of a distinguished member of the judiciary. One old lady, whom I had met before, and who was a notorious gambler, revealed to my secret vision as her repressed complex a gigantic pike. The fish literally swam in the air over the dame's head, darting every now and then ferociously at prey invisible to me.

"I hear," observed Pawkins at last, "that there is a case of plague in quarantine."

The wolf leered over his shoulder and licked its hideous jaw. The introduction of so dire a theme at that crisis in my life spoiled the dinner for me. I listened to the flow of talk about me, hearing much speculation regarding such things as fleas and the bacilli. Mrs. Lancaster seemed only half aware of what was transpiring around her. My attention was drawn particularly to her by the suggestion of a wraith upon her shoulder. I had looked eagerly in her direction more than once, hoping to descry the symbolized embodiment of her complex. That there was a form of some description outlined upon her shoulder seemed clear. I thought at first it might be a bird. Later it wore the aspect of a fish. At last, I had to abandon the effort to define to myself the shadowy thing moving from her right arm around her shoulders to her left. The secret of my patient's repressed complex was almost mine. Again and again it eluded me. The vexation of that circumstance made the end of the dinner a welcome relief. I strolled into the smoking room, listening vaguely to the din of the violins, tuning for the dance.

Finding myself alone, I peered into my pocket. Philander was fast asleep. I hated to disturb the repose of the golden creature, and for that reason remained with my cigar alone to the last possible minute. In the end I was obliged to make my appearance in the ballroom.

There was not a dancer on the whole vast floor without his or her attendant creature. A member of the United States Senate was closely followed in the mazes of a waltz by an opossum, while his partner, a lady with some fame as a landscape painter, kept a porcupine in her train. The pastor of a church led a vampire in its flight among the dancers, above whom it poised itself, fanning sundry individuals with its wings. There was one gigantic crocodile in a corner which every now and then abandoned the shelter of the wall to cavort and caper after the founder of fifteen hospitals. In short, wherever I looked I beheld specimens of a zoology unsuspected by those who danced in and about among pelicans, pumas, guinea pigs and polar bears. One gigantic creature, symbolizing the repressed complex of the most

famous lawyer in the country, was evidently an antedi-
luvian monster. It appeared to my astonished gaze
somewhat like a lepidosiren. These creatures were like
the men and women they all haunted in turning, twisting and waltzing to the music. Now and then there were
collisions of a significant sort. I beheld a fierce fight between two bantam roosters, one being the repressed
complex of a well known novelist and the other that of
a successful merchant. The repressed complex of the
merchant's wife—a lily white hen—watched the struggle complacently. When the bird symbolizing her husband was routed from the field, I saw the lady begin a
fresh dance with the novelist.

It occurred to me to seek my hostess. She had not appeared on the floor for some time. I felt an uneasy
movement in the pocket of my coat. For the sake of
Philander rather than to secure any repose for myself, I
sought the shelter of the Japanese room. I was quite
alone when I sank back wearily upon a sofa and looked
at my watch. It would soon be time to go.

I was opening my cigarette case when Mrs. Lancaster
appeared in the doorway. Her exquisite features wore an
unusual gravity, even for her, as she advanced. I divined
that she had a revelation to make. Whatever I might
have said remained unspoken, however, in the shock of
discovering a golden rat perched upon her shoulder. For
a moment the idea entered my head that Philander must
have escaped from my pocket. I perceived, as soon as I
had looked at the creature again, that I could not implicate Philander. The golden rat on the shoulder of Mrs.
Lancaster was smaller than my pet. It was of less robust
physique, softer in outline, more graceful.

I had placed my hand in Mrs. Lancaster's outstretched fingers, when a flashing form sprang from the
pocket of my coat. There was a tiny shriek of joy. I saw
Philander capering and shrieking on the floor with the

diminutive creature that followed him from the shoulders of the lady who had so long been my most baffling patient.

"I think," I managed to say, my eyes riveted upon the gamboling creatures on the floor—"I think I have the key to your case."

I saw a flush spread from her cheek to her brow. She bowed her head and, still holding my hand, sank upon the chair from which I had just risen. It seems odd to me, as I look back upon all this, that I never suspected the mutual infatuation out of which our repressed complexes were built up. She loved me. I saw the avowal in the eyes she turned up to my face as I bent over her. As our lips met, I felt a convulsive shudder at my breast. I put my hand in my coat. There lay Philander.

To my profound amazement, the rat bit me. With an effort, I repressed an exclamation of pain. Thrusting the little creature, who seemed disposed to escape, back into my pocket, I literally fled the place.

There was no one stirring as I entered my dark study and turned on the light. How long I sat absorbed in my reflections I knew not. There was a patch of crimson in the sky when at last I got up from my desk and walked over to the window.

How long had this woman loved me? Through what circumstance had it become possible for her to identify me with the golden rat? I was, evidently, her repressed complex. As I stood at the window pondering these things, a figure moved across the lawn.

"Boggs!" I called.

It was that honest hostler. He had just set about the business of the stables.

"Have you seen Mrs. Lancaster?"

"She was here to see you last month, sir."

"Why was I not told?"

"Why, sir, I thought the girl would tell you. She waited for you here an hour. She saw the golden rat."

"You mean," I interrupted, "that you showed it to her."

"I told her how fond of it you had grown, sir."

Here then was the explanation I sought. The mention of the golden rat reminded me at once of Philander. I had quite forgotten, in the bewilderment resulting from my experience with Mrs. Lancaster, to shut him up for the night in his cage.

"Philander!"

I called him again and again without effect.

"Boggs," I remarked, "do you remember when Doctor Graham was here to set his traps?"

The stableman scratched his head with a most aggravating stupidity. Yes, he remembered the visit of the physician. He recalled the setting of the traps. He had not seen them placed. He did not know where they were. I lost no time in getting to the stables with a lantern. The search was fruitless. There were no traps that I could discover. Boggs remembered that the old doctor had talked of the cellar. Thither we repaired. I found no traps. The failure to discover the devices did not console me in the least. I knew the old doctor to be a cunning and experienced rat catcher. He might have hidden his deadly devices under a loose plank or in a remote closet.

The full dawn of that morning brought no Philander. I ransacked the house without avail. Neither trap nor rat resulted. The day following was but a repetition of the disappointment. I discovered to my dismay that Doctor Graham had left the city for a few days. The official of the Board of Health to whom I telephoned offered to send an inspector to my house at once. The doctor had left at headquarters a list of every domicile in which a trap was set. I closed with the offer immediately. The result was another vain search of my premises.

The despair to which I was reduced by the continued

disappearance of Philander led me to overlook, at the time, a curious circumstance connected with Thorburn. I saw him for a brief interval on the street. He was not accompanied by the ghostly stork. The detail made no impression upon my mind for an hour or more after I had parted from him. Then I hurried to the street. A week before, I would have beheld the repressed complex of any passerby. Now I saw dozens of pedestrians. No beast or bird attended any.

Turning back into the house with a strange giddiness in my head, I was halted by the arrival before my door of a motor car. Out stepped old Graham.

"The trap!" I shouted. "Where did you set it?"

I observed that no dove fluttered about him now.

"The trap?" he echoed. "In your study, of course."

I staggered after him. He led the way to a corner of a bookcase into which I had not once dreamed of peering. With loud triumph, the old doctor lifted a trap on high. It held Philander, cold and dead.

"Very, very remarkable," he observed. "Wouldn't you say this rat has a golden color?"

His face reflected a grave anxiety. I spoke up savagely:

"It's a golden rat. Are you afraid of it—it is dead."

"I hear you've been looking for me," he said, wiping his eyes with a handkerchief. "I was called out of town by the case of Mrs. Lancaster."

"Is she ill?"

He lifted the dead form of Philander from the trap before replying:

"Her people had her committed to a sanitarium. She insists that she is followed everywhere by a golden rat."

A GRAMMATICAL GHOST

Elia W. Peattie

T here was only one possible objection to the
drawing-room, and that was the occasional presence of Miss Carew; and only one possible objection to Miss Carew. And that was, that she was dead.

She had been dead twenty years, as a matter of fact
and record, and to the last of her life sacredly preserved
the treasures and traditions of her family, a family
bound up—as it is quite unnecessary to explain to any
one in good society—with all that is more venerable
and heroic in the history of the Republic. Miss Carew
never relaxed the proverbial hospitality of her house,
even when she remained its sole representative. She
continued to preside at her table with dignity and state,
and to set an example of excessive modesty and gentle
decorum to a generation of restless young women.

It is not likely that having lived a life of such irre-
proachable gentility as this, Miss Carew would have the
bad taste to die in any way not pleasant to mention in

fastidious society. She could be trusted to the last, not to outrage those friends who quoted her as an exemplar of propriety. She died very unobtrusively of an affection of the heart, one June morning, while trimming her rose trellis, and her lavender-colored print was not even rumpled when she fell, nor were more than the tips of her little bronze slippers visible.

"Isn't it dreadful," said the Philadelphians, "that the property should go to a very, very distant cousin in Iowa or somewhere else on the frontier, about whom nobody knows anything at all?"

The Carew treasures were packed in boxes and sent away into the Iowa wilderness; the Carew traditions were preserved by the Historical Society; the Carew property, standing in one of the most umbrageous and aristocratic suburbs of Philadelphia, was rented to all manner of folk—anybody who had money enough to pay the rental—and society entered its doors no more.

But at last, after twenty years, and when all save the oldest Philadelphians had forgotten Miss Lydia Carew, the very, very distant cousin appeared. He was quite in the prime of life, and so agreeable and unassuming that nothing could be urged against him save his patronymic, which, being Boggs, did not commend itself to the euphemists. With him were two maiden sisters, ladies of excellent taste and manners, who restored the Carew china to its ancient cabinets, and replaced the Carew pictures upon the walls, with additions not out of keeping with the elegance of these heirlooms. Society, with a magnanimity almost dramatic, overlooked the name of Boggs—and called.

All was well. At least, to an outsider all seemed to be well. But, in truth, there was a certain distress in the old mansion, and in the hearts of the well-behaved Misses Boggs. It came about most unexpectedly. The sisters had been sitting upstairs, looking out at the beautiful grounds of the old place, and marvelling at the violets, which lifted their heads from every possible cranny about the house, and talking over the cordiality which they had been receiving by those upon whom they had no claim, and they were filled with amiable satisfaction. Life looked attractive. They had often been grateful to Miss Lydia Carew for leaving their brother her fortune. Now they felt even more grateful to her. She had left them a Social Position—one, which even after twenty years of desuetude, was fit for use.

They descended the stairs together, with arms clasped about each other's waists, and as they did so presented a placid and pleasing sight. They entered their drawing room with the intention of brewing a cup of tea, and drinking it in calm sociability in the twilight. But as they entered the room they became aware of the presence of a lady, who was already seated at their tea-table, regarding their old Wedgwood with the air of a connoisseur.

There were a number of peculiarities about this intruder. To begin with, she was hatless, quite as if she were a habitué of the house, and was costumed in a prim lilac-colored lawn of the style of two decades past. But a greater peculiarity was the resemblance this lady bore to a faded Daguerrotype. If looked at one way, she was perfectly discernible; if looked at another, she went out in a sort of blur. Notwithstanding this comparative invisibility, she exhaled a delicate perfume of sweet lavender, very pleasing to the nostrils of the Misses Boggs, who stood looking at her in gentle and unprotesting surprise.

"I beg your pardon," began Miss Prudence, the younger of the Misses Boggs, "but—"

But at this moment the Daguerrotype became a blur, and Miss Prudence found herself addressing space. The Misses Boggs were irritated. They had never encountered any mysteries in Iowa. They began an impatient search behind doors and portières, and even under sofas, though it was quite absurd to suppose that a lady recognizing the merits of the Carew Wedgwood would so far forget herself as to crawl under a sofa.

When they had given up all hope of discovering the intruder, they saw her standing at the far end of the drawing-room critically examining a water-color marine. The elder Miss Boggs started toward her with stern decision, but the little Daguerrotype turned with a shadowy smile, became a blur and an imperceptibility.

Miss Boggs looked at Miss Prudence Boggs.

"If there were ghosts," she said, "this would be one."

"If there were ghosts," said Miss Prudence Boggs, "this would be the ghost of Lydia Carew."

The twilight was settling into blackness, and Miss Boggs nervously lit the gas while Miss Prudence ran for other tea-cups, preferring, for reasons superfluous to mention, not to drink out of the Carew china that evening.

The next day, on taking up her embroidery frame, Miss Boggs found a number of old-fashioned cross-stitches added to her Kensington. Prudence, she knew, would never have degraded herself by taking a cross-stitch, and the parlor-maid was above taking such a liberty. Miss Boggs mentioned the incident that night at a dinner given by an ancient friend of the Carews.

"Oh, that's the work of Lydia Carew, without a doubt!" cried the hostess. "She visits every new family that moves to the house, but she never remains more than a week or two with any one."

"It must be that she disapproves of them," suggested Miss Boggs.

"I think that's it," said the hostess. "She doesn't like their china, or their fiction."

"I hope she'll disapprove of us," added Miss Prudence.

The hostess belonged to a very old Philadelphian family, and she shook her head.

"I should say it was a compliment for even the ghost of Miss Lydia Carew to approve of one," she said severely.

The next morning, when the sisters entered their drawing-room there were numerous evidences of an occupant during their absence. The sofa pillows had been rearranged so that the effect of their grouping was less bizarre than that favored by the Western women; a horrid little Buddhist idol with its eyes fixed on its abdomen, had been chastely hidden behind a Dresden shepherdess, as unfit for the scrutiny of polite eyes; and on the table where Miss Prudence did work in water colors, after the fashion of the impressionists, lay a prim and impossible composition representing a moss-rose and a number of heartsease, colored with that caution which modest spinster artists instinctively exercise.

"Oh, there's no doubt it's the work of Miss Lydia Carew," said Miss Prudence, contemptuously. "There's no mistaking the drawing of that rigid little rose. Don't you remember those wreaths and bouquets framed, among the pictures we got when the Carew pictures were sent to us? I gave some of them to an orphan asylum and burned up the rest."

"Hush!" cried Miss Boggs, involuntarily. "If she heard you, it would hurt her feelings terribly. Of course, I mean—" and she blushed. "It might hurt her feelings—but how perfectly ridiculous! It's impossible!"

Miss Prudence held up the sketch of the moss-rose.

"*That* may be impossible in an artistic sense, but it is a palpable thing."

"Bosh!" cried Miss Boggs.

"But," protested Miss Prudence, "how do you explain it?"

"I don't," said Miss Boggs, and left the room.

That evening the sisters made a point of being in the drawing-room before the dusk came on, and of lighting the gas at the first hint of twilight. They didn't believe in Miss Lydia Carew—but still they meant to be beforehand with her. They talked with unwonted vivacity and in a louder tone than was their custom. But as they drank their tea even their utmost verbosity could not make them oblivious to the fact that the perfume of sweet lavender was stealing insidiously through the room. They tacitly refused to recognize this odor and all that it indicated, when suddenly, with a sharp crash, one of the old Carew teacups fell from the tea-table to the floor and was broken. The disaster was followed by what sounded like a sigh of pain and dismay.

"I didn't suppose Miss Lydia Carew would ever be as awkward as that," cried the younger Miss Boggs, petulantly.

"Prudence," said her sister with a stern accent, "please try not to be a fool. You brushed the cup off with the sleeve of your dress."

"Your theory wouldn't be so bad," said Miss Prudence, half laughing and half crying, "if there were any sleeves to my dress, but, as you see, there aren't," and then Miss Prudence had something as near hysterics as a healthy young woman from the West can have.

"I wouldn't think such a perfect lady as Lydia Carew," she ejaculated between her sobs, "would make herself so disagreeable! You may talk about good-breeding all you please, but I call such intrusion exceedingly bad taste. I have a horrible idea that she likes us and means to stay with us. She left those other people because she did not approve of their habits or their grammar. It would be just our luck to please her."

"Well, I like your egotism," said Miss Boggs.

However, the view Miss Prudence took of the case appeared to be the right one. Time went by and Miss Lydia Carew still remained. When the ladies entered their drawing-room they would see the little lady-like Daguerrotype revolving itself into a blur before one of the family portraits. Or they noticed that the yellow sofa cushion, toward which she appeared to feel a peculiar antipathy, had been dropped behind the sofa upon the floor; or that one of Jane Austen's novels, which none of the family ever read, had been removed from the book shelves and left open upon the table.

"I cannot become reconciled to it," complained Miss Boggs to Miss Prudence. "I wish we had remained in Iowa where we belong. Of course I don't believe in the thing! No sensible person would. But still I cannot become reconciled."

But their liberation was to come, and in a most unexpected manner.

A relative by marriage visited them from the West. He was a friendly man and had much to say, so he talked all through dinner, and afterward followed the ladies to the drawing-room to finish his gossip. The gas in the room was turned very low, and as they entered Miss Prudence caught sight of Miss Carew, in company attire, sitting in upright propriety in a stiff-backed chair at the extremity of the apartment.

Miss Prudence had a sudden idea.

"We will not turn up the gas," she said, with an emphasis intended to convey private information to her sister. "It will be more agreeable to sit here and talk in this soft light."

Neither her brother nor the man from the West made any objection. Miss Boggs and Miss Prudence, clasping each other's hands, divided their attention between their corporeal and their incorporeal guests. Miss Boggs was confident that her sister had an idea, and was willing to await its development. As the guest from Iowa spoke, Miss Carew bent a politely attentive ear to what he said.

"Ever since Richards took sick that time," he said briskly, "it seemed like he shed all responsibility." (The Misses Boggs saw the Daguerrotype put up her shadowy head with a movement of doubt and apprehension.) "The fact of the matter was, Richards didn't seem to scarcely get on the way he might have been expected to." (At this conscienceless split to the infinitive and misplacing of the preposition, Miss Carew arose trembling perceptibly.) "I saw it wasn't no use for him to count on a quick recovery—"

The Misses Boggs lost the rest of the sentence, for at the utterance of the double negative Miss Lydia Carew had flashed out, not in a blur, but with mortal haste, as when life goes out at a pistol shot!

The man from the West wondered why Miss Prudence should have cried at so pathetic a part of his story:

"Thank Goodness!"

And their brother was amazed to see Miss Boggs kiss Miss Prudence with passion and energy.

It was the end. Miss Carew returned no more.

THE AFFAIR AT
GROVER STATION

Willa Cather

I heard this story sitting on the rear platform of an accommodation freight that crawled along through the brown, sun-dried wilderness between Grover Station and Cheyenne. The narrator was 'Terrapin' Rodgers, who had been a classmate of mine at Princeton, and who was then cashier in the B— railroad office at Cheyenne. Rodgers was an Albany boy, but after his father failed in business, his uncle got 'Terrapin' a position on a Western railroad, and he left college and disappeared completely from out little world, and it was not until I was sent West, by the University with a party of geologists who were digging for fossils in the region about Sterling, Colorado, that I saw him again. On this particular occasion Rodgers had been down at Sterling to spend Sunday with me, and I accompanied him when he returned to Cheyenne.

When the train pulled out of Grover Station, we were sitting smoking on the rear platform, watching the pale yellow disc of the moon that was just rising and that drenched the naked, grey plains in a soft lemon-coloured light. The telegraph poles scored the sky like a musical staff as they flashed by, and the stars, seen between the wires, looked like the notes of some erratic symphony. The stillness of the night and the loneliness and barrenness of the plains were conducive to an uncanny train of thought. We had just left Grover Station behind us, and the murder of the station agent at Grover, which had occurred the previous winter, was still the subject of much conjecturing and theorising all along that line or railroad. Rodgers had been an intimate friend of the murdered agent, and it was said that he knew more about the affair than any other living man, but with that peculiar reticence which at college had won him the soubriquet 'Terrapin', he had kept what he knew to himself, and even the most accomplished reporter on the *New York Journal*, who had travelled half-way across the continent for the express purpose of pumping Rodgers, had given him up as impossible. But I had known Rodgers a long time, and since I had been grubbing in the chalk about Sterling, we had fallen into a habit of exchanging confidences, for it is good to see an old face in a strange land. So, as the little red station house at Grover faded into the distance, I asked him point blank what he knew about the murder of Lawrence O'Toole. Rodgers took a long pull at his black-briar pipe as he answered me.

'Well, yes. I could tell you something about it, but the question is how much you'd believe, and whether you could restrain yourself from reporting it to the Society for Psychical Research. I never told the story but once, and then it was to the Division Superintendent, and when I finished the old gentleman asked if I were a drinking man, and remarking that a fertile imagination was not a desirable quality in a railroad employee, said it would be just as well if the story went no further. You see it's a gruesome tale, and someway we don't like to be reminded that there are more things in heaven and earth than our systems of philosophy can grapple with. However, I should rather like to tell the story to a man who would look at it objectively and leave it in the domain of pure incident where it belongs. It would unburden my mind, and I'd like to get a scientific man's opinion on the yarn. But I suppose I'd better begin at the beginning, with the dance which preceded the tragedy, just as such things follow each other in a play. I notice that Destiny, who is a good deal of an artist in her way, frequently falls back upon that elementary principle of contrast to make things interesting for us.

'It was the thirty-first of December, the morning of the incoming Governor's inaugural ball, and I got down to the office early, for I had a heavy day's work ahead of me, and I was going to the dance and wanted to close up by six o'clock. I had scarcely unlocked the door when I heard someone calling Cheyenne on the wire, and hurried over to the instrument to see what was wanted. It was Lawrence O'Toole, at Grover, and he said he was coming up for the ball on the extra, due in Cheyenne at nine o'clock that night. He wanted me to go up to see Miss Masterson and ask her if she could go with him. He had had some trouble in getting leave of absence, as the last regular train for Cheyenne then left Grover at 5:45 in the afternoon, and as there was an east-bound going through Grover at 7:30, the dispatcher didn't want him array, in case there should be orders for the 7:30 train. So Larry had made no arrangement with Miss Masterson, as he was uncertain about getting up until he was notified about the extra.

'I telephoned Miss Masterson and delivered Larry's message. She replied that she had made an arrangement to go to the dance with Mr Freymark, but added laughingly that no other arrangement held when Larry could come.

'About noon Freymark dropped in at the office, and I suspected he'd got his time from Miss Masterson. While he was hanging around, Larry called me up to tell me that Helen's flowers would be up from Denver on the Union Pacific passenger at five, and he asked me to have them sent up to her promptly and to call for her that evening in case the extra should be late. Freymark, of course, listened to the message, and when the sounder stopped, he smiled in a slow, disagreeable way, and saying, "Thank you. That's all I wanted to know." left the office.

'Lawrence O'Toole had been my predecessor in the cashier's office at Cheyenne, and he needs a little explanation now that he is under ground, though when he was in the world of living men, he explained himself better than any man I have ever met, East or West. I've knocked about a good deal since I cut loose from Princeton, and I've found that there are a great many good fellows in the world, but I've not found many better than Larry. I think I can say, without stretching a point, that he was the most popular man on the Division. He had a faculty of making everyone like him that amounted to a sort of genius. When he first went to working on the road, he was the agent's assistant down at Sterling, a mere kid fresh from Ireland, without a dollar in his pocket, and no sort of backing in the world but his quick wit and handsome face. It was a face that served him as a sight draft, good in all banks.

'Freymark was cashier at the Cheyenne office then, but he had been up to some dirty work with the company, and when it fell in the line of Larry's duty to expose him, he did so without hesitating. Eventually Freymark was discharged, and Larry was made cashier in his place. There was, after that, naturally, little love lost between them, and to make matters worse, Helen Masterson took a fancy to Larry, and Freymark had begun to consider himself pretty solid in that direction. I doubt whether Miss Masterson ever really liked the blackguard, but he was a queer fish, and she was a queer girl and she found him interesting.

'Old John J. Masterson, her father, had been United States Senator from Wyoming, and Helen had been educated at Wellesley and had lived in Washington a good deal. She found Cheyenne dull and had got into the Washington way of tolerating anything but stupidity, and Freymark certainly was not stupid. He passed as an Alsatian Jew, but he had lived a good deal in Paris and had been pretty much all over the world, and spoke the more general European languages fluently. He was a wiry, sallow, unwholesome looking man, slight and meagrely built, and he looked as though he had been dried through and through by the blistering heat of the tropics. His movements were as lithe and agile as those of a cat, and invested with a certain, stealthy grace. His eyes were small and black as bright jet beads; his hair very thick and coarse and straight, black with a sort of purple lustre to it, and he always wore it correctly parted in the middle and brushed smoothly about his ears. He had a pair of the most impudent red lips that closed over white, regular teeth. His hands, of which he took the greatest care, were the yellow, wrinkled hands of an old man, and shrivelled at the finger tips, though I don't think he could have been much over thirty. The long and short of it is that the fellow was uncanny. You somehow felt that there was that in his present, or in his past, or in his destiny which isolated him from other men. He dressed in excellent taste, was always accommodating, with the most polished manners and an address extravagantly deferential. He went into cattle after he lost his job with the company and had an interest in a ranch ten miles out, though he spent most of his time in Cheyenne at the Capitol card rooms. He had an insatiable passion for gambling, and he was one of the few men who make it pay.

'About a week before the dance, Larry's cousin, Harry Burns, who was a reporter on the London *Times*, stopped in Cheyenne on his way to 'Frisco, and Larry came up to meet him. We took Burns up to the club, and I noticed that he acted rather queerly when Freymark came in. Burns went down to Grover to spend a day with Larry, and on Saturday Larry wired me to come down and spend Sunday with him, as he had important news for me.

'I went, and the gist of his information was that Freymark, then going by another name, had figured in a particularly ugly London scandal that happened to be in Burns' beat, and his record had been exposed. He was, indeed, from Paris, but there was not a drop of Jewish blood in his veins, and he dated from farther back than Israel. His father was a French soldier who, during his service in the East, had bought a Chinese slave girl, had become attached to her, and married her, and after her death had brought her child back to Europe with him. He had entered the civil service and held several subordinate offices in the capital, where his son was educated. The boy, socially ambitious and extremely sensitive about his Asiatic blood, after having been blackballed at a club, had left and lived by an exceedingly questionable traffic in London, assuming a Jewish patronymic to account for his Oriental complexion and traits of feature. That explained everything. That explained why Freymark's hands were those of a centenarian. In his veins crept the sluggish amphibious blood of a race that was already old when Jacob tended the flocks of Laban upon the hills of Padan-Aram, a race that was in its mort cloth before Europe's swaddling clothes were made.

'Of course, the question at once came up as to what ought to be done with Burns' information. Cheyenne clubs are not exclusive, but a Chinaman who had been engaged in Freymark's peculiarly unsavoury traffic would be disbarred in almost any region outside of Whitechapel. One thing was sure: Miss Masterson must be informed of the matter at once.

' "On second thought," said Larry, "I guess I'd better tell her myself. It will have to be done easy like, not to hurt her self-respect too much. Like as not I'll go off my head the first time I see him and call him rat-eater to his face."

'Well to get back to the day of the dance, I was wondering whether Larry would stay over to tell Miss Masterson about it the next day, for of course he couldn't spring such a thing on a girl at a party.

'That evening I dressed early and went down to the station at nine to meet Larry. The extra came in, but no Larry. I saw Connelly, the conductor, and asked him if he had seen anything of O'Toole, but he said he hadn't, that the station at Grover was open when he came through, but that he found no train orders and couldn't raise anyone, so he supposed O'Toole had come up on 153. I went back to the office and called Grover, but got no answer. Then I sat down at the instrument and called for fifteen minutes straight. I wanted to go then and hunt up the conductor on 153, the passenger that went through Grover at 5:30 in the afternoon, and ask him what he knew about Larry, but it was then 9:45 and I knew Miss Masterson would be waiting, so I jumped into the carriage and told the driver to make up time.

On my way to the Mastersons' I did some tall thinking. I could find no explanation for O'Toole's non-appearance, but the business of the moment was to invent one for Miss Masterson that would neither alarm nor offend her. I couldn't exactly tell her he wasn't coming, for he might show up yet, so I decided to say the extra was late, and I didn't know when it would be in.

'Miss Masterson had been an exceptionally beautiful girl to begin with, and life had done a great deal for her. Fond as I was of Larry, I used to wonder whether a girl who had led such a full and independent existence would ever find the courage to face life with a railroad man who was so near the bottom of a ladder that is so long and steep.

'She came down the stairs in one of her Paris gowns that are as meat and drink to Cheyenne society reporters, with her arms full of American Beauty roses and her eyes and cheeks glowing. I noticed the roses then, though I didn't know that they were the boy's last message to the woman he loved. She paused half-way down the stairs and looked at me, and then over my head into the drawing-room, and then her eyes questioned mine. I bungled at my explanation and she thanked me for coming, but she couldn't hide her disappointment, and scarcely glanced at herself in the mirror as I put her wrap about her shoulders.

'It was not a cheerful ride down to the Capitol. Miss Masterson did her duty by me bravely, but I found it difficult to be even decently attentive to what she was saying. Once arrived at Representative Hall, where the dance was held, the strain was relieved, for the fellows all pounced on her for dances, and there were friends of hers there from Helena and Laramie, and my responsibility was practically at an end. Don't expect me to tell you what a Wyoming inaugural ball is like. I'm not good at that sort of thing, and this dance is merely incidental to my story. Dance followed dance, and still no Larry. The dances I had with Miss Masterson were torture. She began to question and cross-question me, and when I got tangled up in my lies, she became indignant. Freymark was late in arriving. It must have been after midnight when he appeared, correct and smiling, having driven up from his ranch. He was effusively gay and insisted upon shaking hands with me, though I never willingly touched those clammy hands of his. He was constantly dangling about Miss Masterson, who made rather a point of being gracious to him. I couldn't much blame her under the circumstances, but it irritated me, and I'm not ashamed to say that I rather spied on them. When they were on the balcony I heard him say:

' "You see I've forgotten this morning entirely."

'She answered him rather coolly:

' "Ah, but you are constitutionally forgiving. However, I'll be fair and forgive too. It's more comfortable."

'Then he said in a slow, insinuating tone, and I could fairly see him thrust out those impudent red lips of his as he said it: "If I can teach you to forgive, I wonder whether I could not also teach you to forget? I almost think I could. At any rate I shall make you remember this night.

> *Rappelles-toi lorsque les destinées*
> *M'auront de toi pour jamas séparé."*

'As they came in, I saw him slip one of Larry's red roses into his pocket.

'It was not until near the end of the dance that the clock of destiny sounded the first stroke of the tragedy. I remember how gay the scene was, so gay that I had almost forgotten my anxiety in the music, flowers and laughter. The orchestra was playing a waltz, drawing the strains out long and sweet like the notes of a flute, and Freymark was dancing with Helen. I was not dancing myself then, and suddenly noticed some confusion among the waiters who stood watching by one of the doors, and Larry's black dog, Duke, all foam at the mouth, shot in the side and bleeding, dashed in through the door and eluding the caterer's men, ran half the length of the hall and threw himself at Freymark's feet, uttering a howl piteous enough to herald any sort of calamity. Freymark, who had not seen him before, turned with an exclamation of rage and a face absolutely livid and kicked the wounded brute half-way across the slippery floor. There was something fiendishly brutal and horrible in the episode, it was the breaking out of the barbarian blood through his mask of European civilisation, a jet of black mud that spurted up from some nameless pest hole of filthy heathen cities. The music stopped, people began moving about in a confused mass, and I saw Helen's eyes seeking mine appealingly. I hurried to her, and by the time I reached her Freymark had disappeared.

' "Get the carriage and take care of Duke," she said, and her voice trembled like that of one shivering with cold.

'When we were in the carriage, she spread one of the robes on her knee, and I lifted the dog up to her, and she took him in her arms, comforting him.

' "Where is Larry, and what does all this mean?" she asked. "You can't put me off any longer, for I danced with a man who came up on the extra."

"Then I made a clean breast of it, and told her what I knew, which was little enough.

' "Do you think he is ill?" she asked.

'I replied, "I don't know what to think. I'm all at sea,"—For since the appearance of the dog I was genuinely alarmed.

'She was silent for a long time, but when the rays of the electric street lights flashed at intervals into the carriage, I could see that she was leaning back with her eyes closed and the dog's nose against her throat. At last she said with a note of entreaty in her voice, "Can't you think of anything?" I saw that she was thoroughly frightened and told her that it would probably all end in a joke, and that I would telephone her as soon as I heard from Larry, and would more than likely have something amusing to tell her.

'It was snowing hard when we reached the Senator's, and when we got out of the carriage she gave Duke tenderly over to me and I remember how she dragged on my arm and how played out and exhausted she seemed.

' "You really must not worry at all," I said. "You know how uncertain railroad men are. It's sure to be better at the next inaugural ball; we'll all be dancing together then."

' "The next inaugural ball," she said as we went up the steps, putting out her hand to catch the snowflakes.—"That seems a long way off."

'I got down to the office late next morning, and before I had time to try Grover, the dispatcher at Holyoke called me up to ask whether Larry were still in Cheyenne. He couldn't raise Grover, he said, and he wanted to give Larry train orders for 151, the east-bound passenger. When he heard what I had to say, he told me I had better go down to Grover on 151 myself, as the storm threatened to tie up all the trains and we might look for trouble.

'I had the veterinary surgeon fix up Duke's side, and I put him in the express car, and boarded the 151 with a mighty cold, uncomfortable sensation in the region of my diaphragm.

'It had snowed all night long, and the storm had developed into a blizzard, and the passenger had difficulty in making any headway at all.

'When we got into Grover I thought it was the most desolate spot I had ever looked on, and as the train pulled out, leaving me there, I felt like sending a message of farewell to the world. You know what Grover is, a red box of a station, section house barricaded by coal sheds and a little group of dwellings at the end of everything, with the desert running out on every side to the sky line. The houses and the station were covered with a coating of snow that clung to them like a wet plaster, and the siding was one deep snow drift, banked against the station door. The plain was a wide, white ocean of swirling, drifting snow, that beat and broke like the thrash of the waves in the merciless wind that swept, with nothing to break it, from the Rockies to the Missouri.

'When I opened the station door, the snow fell in upon the floor, and Duke sat down by the empty, fireless stove and began to howl and whine in a heartbreaking fashion. Larry's sleeping room upstairs was empty. Downstairs, everything was in order, and all the station work had been done up. Apparently the last thing Larry had done was to bill out a car of wool from the Oasis sheep ranch for Dewey, Gould & Co., Boston. The car had gone out on 153, the east-bound that left Grover at seven o'clock the night before, so he must have been there at that time. I copied the bill in the copy book, and went over to the section house to make inquiries.

'The section boss was getting ready to go out to look after his track. He said he had seen O'Toole at 5:30, when the west-bound passenger went through, and, not having seen him since, supposed he was still in Cheyenne. I went over to Larry's boarding house, and the woman said he must be in Cheyenne, as he had eaten his supper at five o'clock the night before, so that he would have time to get his station work done and dress. The little girl, she said, had gone over at five to tell him that supper was ready. I questioned the child carefully. She said there was another man, a stranger, in the station with Larry when she went in and that though she didn't hear anything they said, and Larry was sitting with his chair tilted back and his feet on the stove, she somehow had thought they were quarrelling. The stranger, she said, was standing; he had a fur coat on and his eyes snapped like he was mad, and she was afraid of him. I asked her if she could recall anything else about him, and she said, "Yes, he had very red lips." When I heard that, my heart grew cold as a snow lump, and when I went out the wind seemed to go clear through me. It was evident enough that Freymark had gone down there to make trouble, had quarrelled with Larry and had boarded either the 5:30 passenger or the extra, and got the conductor to let him off at his ranch, and accounted for his late appearance at the dance.

'It was five o'clock then, but the 5:30 train was two hours late, so there was nothing to do but sit down and wait for the conductor, who had gone out on the seven o'clock east-bound the night before, and who must have seen Larry when he picked up the car of wool. It was growing dark by that time. The sky was a dull lead colour, and the snow had drifted about the little town until it was almost buried, and was still coming down so fast that you could scarcely see your hand before you.

'I was never so glad to hear anything as that whistle, when old 153 came lumbering and groaning in through the snow. I ran out on the platform to meet her, and her headlight looked like the face of an old friend. I caught the conductor's arm the minute he stepped off the train, but he wouldn't talk until he got in by the fire. He said he hadn't seen O'Toole at all the night before, but he had found the bill for the wool car on the table, with a note from Larry asking him to take the car out on the Q.T., and he had concluded that Larry had gone up to Cheyenne on the 5:30. I wired the Cheyenne office and managed to catch the express clerk who had gone through on the extra the night before. He wired me saying that he had not seen Larry board the extra, but that his dog had crept into his usual place in the express car, and he had supposed Larry was in the coach. He had seen Freymark get on at Grover, and the train had slowed up a trifle at his ranch to let him off, for Freymark stood in with some of the boys and sent his cattle shipments our way.

'When the night fairly closed down on me, I began to wonder how a gay, expansive fellow like O'Toole had ever stood six months at Grover. The snow had let up by that time, and the stars were beginning to glitter cold and bright through the hurrying clouds. I put on my ulster and went outside. I began a minute tour of inspection, I went through empty freight cars run down by the siding, searched the coal houses and primitive cellar, examining them carefully, and calling O'Toole's name. Duke at my heels dragged himself painfully about, but seemed as much at sea as I, and betrayed the nervous suspense and alertness of a bird dog that has lost his game.

'I went back to the office and took the big station lamp upstairs to make a more careful examination of Larry's sleeping room. The suit of clothes that he usually wore at his work was hanging on the wall. His shaving things were lying about, and I recognised the silver-backed military hair brushes that Miss Masterson had given him at Christmas time, lying on his chiffonier. The upper drawer was open and a pair of white kid gloves was lying on the corner. A white string tie hung across his pipe rack, it was crumpled and had evidently proved unsatisfactory when he tied it. On the chiffonier lay several clean handkerchiefs with holes in them, where he had unfolded them and thrown them by in a hasty search for a whole one. A black silk muffler hung on the chair back, and a top hat was set awry on the head of a plaster cast of Parnell, Larry's hero. His dress suit was missing, so there was no doubt that he had dressed for the party. His overcoat lay on his trunk and his dancing shoes were on the floor, at the foot of the bed beside his everyday ones. I knew that his pumps were a little tight, he had joked about them when I was down the Sunday before the dance, but he had only one pair, and he couldn't have got another in Grover if he had tried himself. That set me to thinking. He was a dainty fellow about his shoes and I knew his collection pretty well. I went to his closet and found them all there. Even granting him a prejudice against overcoats, I couldn't conceive of his going out in that stinging weather without shoes. I noticed that a surgeon's case, such as are carried on passenger trains, and which Larry had once appropriated in Cheyenne, was open, and that the roll of medicated cotton had been pulled out and recently used. Each discovery I made served only to add to my perplexity. Granted that Freymark had been there, and granted that he had played the boy an ugly trick, he could not have spirited him away without the knowledge of the train crew.

' "Duke, old doggy," I said to the poor spaniel who was sniffing and whining about the bed, "you haven't done your duty. You must have seen what went on between your master and that clam-blooded Asiatic, and you ought to be able to give me a tip of some sort."

'I decided to go to bed and make a fresh start on the ugly business in the morning. The bed looked as though someone had been lying on it, so I started to beat it up a little before I got in. I took off the pillow and as I pulled up the mattress, on the edge of the ticking at the head of the bed, I saw a dark red stain about the size of my hand. I felt the cold sweat come out on me, and my hands were dangerously unsteady, as I carried the lamp over and set it down on the chair by the bed. But Duke was too quick for me, he had seen that stain and leaping on the bed began sniffing it, and whining like a dog that is being whipped to death. I bent down and felt it with my fingers. It was dry but the colour and stiffness were unmistakeably those of coagulated blood. I caught up my coat and vest and ran down stairs with Duke yelping at my heels. My first impulse was to go and call someone, but from the platform not a single light was visible, and I knew the section men had been in bed for hours. I remembered then, that Larry was often annoyed by haemorrhages at the nose in that high altitude, but even that did not altogether quiet my nerves, and I realised that sleeping in that bed was quite out of the question.

'Larry always kept a supply of brandy and soda on hand, so I made myself a stiff drink and filled the stove and locked the door, turned down the lamp and lay down on the operator's table. I had often slept there when I was night operator. At first it was impossible to sleep, for Duke kept starting up and limping to the door and scratching at it, yelping nervously. He kept this up until I was thoroughly unstrung, and though I'm ordinarily cool enough, there wasn't money enough in Wyoming to have bribed me to open that door. I felt cold all over every time I went near it, and I even drew the big rusty bolt that was never used, and it seemed to me that it groaned heavily as I drew it, or perhaps it was the wind outside that groaned. As for Duke, I threatened to put him out, and boxed his ears until I hurt his feelings, and he lay down in front of the door with his muzzle between his paws and his eyes shining like live coals and riveted on the crack under the door. The situation was gruesome enough, but the liquor had made me drowsy and at last I fell asleep.

'It must have been about three o'clock in the morning that I was awakened by the crying of the dog, a whimper low, continuous and pitiful, and indescribably human. While I was blinking my eyes in an effort to get thoroughly awake, I heard another sound, the grating sound of chalk on a wooden black board, or of a soft pencil on a slate. I turned my head to the right, and saw a man standing with his back to me, chalking something on the bulletin board. At a glance I recognised the broad, high shoulders and the handsome head of my friend. Yet there was that about the figure which kept me from calling his name or from moving a muscle where I lay. He finished his writing and dropped the chalk, and I distinctly heard its click as it fell. He made a gesture as though he were dusting his fingers, and then turned facing me, holding his left hand in front of his mouth. I saw him clearly in the soft light of the station lamp. He wore his dress clothes, and began moving towards the door silently as a shadow in the black stocking feet. There was about his movements an indescribable stiffness, as though his limbs had been frozen. His face was chalky white, his hair seemed damp and was plastered down close about his temples. His eyes were colourless jellies, dull as lead, and staring straight before him. When he reached the door, he lowered the hand he held before his mouth to lift the latch. His face was turned squarely towards me, and the lower jaw had fallen and was set rigidly upon his collar, the mouth was wide open and was *stuffed full of white cotton*! Then I knew it was a dead man's face I looked upon.

'The door opened, and that stiff black figure in stockings walked as noiselessly as a cat out into the night. I think I went quite mad then. I dimly remember that I rushed out upon the siding and ran up and down screaming, "Larry, Larry!" until the wind seemed to echo my call. The stars were out in myriads, and the snow glistened in their light, but I could see nothing but the wide, white plain, not even a dark shadow anywhere. When at last I found myself back in the station, I saw Duke lying before the door and dropped on my knees beside him, calling him by name. But Duke was past calling back. Master and dog had gone together, and I dragged him into the corner and covered his face, for his eyes were colourless and soft, like the eyes of that horrible face, once so beloved.

'The black board? O, I didn't forget that. I had chalked the time of the accommodation on it the night before, from sheer force of habit, for it isn't customary to mark the time of trains in unimportant stations like Grover. My writing had been rubbed out by a moist hand, for I could see the finger marks clearly, and in place of it was written in blue chalk simply,

C.B. & Q. 26387

'I sat there drinking brandy and muttering to myself before that black board until those blue letters danced up and down, like magic lantern pictures when you jiggle the slides. I drank until the sweat poured off me like rain and my teeth chattered, and I turned sick at the stomach. At last an idea flashed upon me. I snatched the way bill off the hook. The car of wool that had left Grover for Boston the night before was numbered 26387.

'I must have got through the rest of the night somehow, for when the sun came up red and angry over the white plains, the section boss found me sitting by the stove, the lamp burning full blaze, the brandy bottle empty beside me, and with but one idea in my head,

102

that box car 26387 must be stopped and opened as soon as possible, and that somehow it would explain.

'I figured that we could easily catch it in Omaha, and wired the freight agent there to go through it carefully and report anything unusual. That night I got a wire from the agent stating that the body of a man had been found under a woolsack at one end of the car with a fan and an invitation to the inaugural ball at Cheyenne in the pocket of his dress coat. I wired him not to disturb the body until I arrived, and started for Omaha. Before I left Grover the Cheyenne office wired me that Freymark had left town, going west over the Union Pacific. The company detectives never found him.

'The matter was clear enough then. Being a railroad man, he had hidden the body and sealed up the car and billed it out, leaving a note for the conductor. Since he was of a race without conscience or sensibilities, and since his past was more infamous than his birth, he had boarded the extra and had gone to the ball and danced with Miss Masterson with blood undried upon his hands.

'When I saw Larry O'Toole again, he was lying stiff and stark in the undertakers' rooms in Omaha. He was clad in his dress clothes, with black stockings on his feet, as I had seen him forty-eight hours before. Helen Masterson's fan was in his pocket. His mouth was wide open and stuffed full of white cotton.

'He had been shot in the mouth, the bullet lodging between the third and fourth vertebrae. The haemorrhage had been very slight and had been checked by the cotton. The quarrel had taken place about five in the afternoon. After supper Larry had dressed, all but his shoes, and had lain down to snatch a wink of sleep, trusting to the whistle of the extra to waken him. Freymark had gone back and shot him while he was asleep, afterwards placing his body in the wool car, which, but for my telegram, would not have been opened for weeks.

'That's the whole story. There is nothing more to tell except one detail that I did not mention to the superintendent. When I said good-bye to the boy before the undertaker and coroner took charge of the body, I lifted his right hand to take off a ring that Miss Masterson had given him and the ends of the fingers were covered with blue chalk.'

THE DOLL'S GHOST

F. Marion Crawford

It was a terrible accident, and for one moment the splendid machinery of Cranston House got out of gear and stood still. The butler emerged from the retirement in which he spent his elegant leisure, two grooms of the chambers appeared simultaneously from opposite directions, there were actually housemaids on the grand staircase, and those who remember the facts most exactly assert that Mrs. Pringle herself positively stood upon the landing. Mrs. Pringle was the housekeeper. As for the head nurse, the under nurse, and the nursery maid, their feelings cannot be described. The head nurse laid one hand upon the polished marble balustrade and stared stupidly before her, the under nurse stood rigid and pale, leaning against the polished marble wall, and the nursery-maid collapsed and sat down upon the polished marble step, just beyond the limits of the velvet carpet, and frankly burst into tears.

The Lady Gwendolen Lancaster-Douglas-Scroop,

youngest daughter of the ninth Duke of Cranston, and aged six years and three months, picked herself up quite alone, and sat down on the third step from the foot of the grand staircase in Cranston House.

"Oh!" exclaimed the butler, and he disappeared again.

"Ah!" responded the grooms of the chambers, as they also went away.

"It's only that doll," Mrs. Pringle was distinctly heard to say, in a tone of contempt.

The under nurse heard her say it. Then the three nurses gathered round Lady Gwendolen and patted her, and gave her unhealthy things out of their pockets, and hurried her out of Cranston House as fast as they could, lest it should be found out upstairs that they had allowed the Lady Gwendolen Lancaster-Douglas-Scroop to tumble down the grand staircase with her doll in her arms. And as the doll was badly broken, the nursery-maid carried it, with the pieces, wrapped up in Lady Gwendolen's little cloak. It was not far to Hyde Park, and when they had reached a quiet place they took means to find out that Lady Gwendolen had no bruises. For the carpet was very thick and soft, and there was thick stuff under it to make it softer.

Lady Gwendolen Douglas-Scroop sometimes yelled, but she never cried. It was because she had yelled that the nurse had allowed her to go downstairs alone with Nina, the doll, under one arm, while she steadied herself with her other hand on the balustrade, and trod upon the polished marble steps beyond the edge of the carpet. So she had fallen, and Nina had come to grief.

When the nurses were quite sure that she was not hurt, they unwrapped the doll and looked at her in turn. She had been a very beautiful doll, very large, and fair, and healthy, with real yellow hair, and eyelids that would open and shut over very grown-up dark eyes.

Moreover, when you moved her right arm up and down she said "Pa-pa," and when you moved the left she said, "Ma-ma," very distinctly.

"I heard her say 'Pa' when she fell," said the under nurse, who heard everything. "But she ought to have said 'Pa-pa.'"

"That's because her arm went up when she hit the step," said the head nurse. "She'll say the other 'Pa' when I put it down again."

"Pa," said Nina, as her right arm was pushed down, and speaking through her broken face. It was cracked right across, from the upper corner of the forehead, with a hideous gash, through the nose and down to the little frilled collar of the pale green silk Mother Hubbard frock, and two little three-cornered pieces of porcelain had fallen out.

"I'm sure it's a wonder she can speak at all, being all smashed," said the under nurse.

"You'll have to take her to Mr. Puckler," said her superior. "It's not far, and you'd better go at once."

Lady Gwendolen was occupied in digging a hole in the ground with a little spade, and paid no attention to the nurses.

"What are you doing?" enquired the nursery-maid, looking on.

"Nina's dead, and I'm diggin' her a grave," replied her ladyship thoughtfully.

"Oh, she'll come to life again all right," said the nursery-maid.

The under nurse wrapped Nina up again and departed. Fortunately a kind soldier, with very long legs and a very small cap, happened to be there; and as he had nothing to do, he offered to see the under nurse safely to Mr. Puckler's and back.

* * *

107

BODIES OF THE DEAD

Mr. Bernard Puckler and his little daughter lived in a little house in a little alley, which led out off a quiet little street not very far from Belgrave Square. He was the great doll doctor, and his extensive practice lay in the most aristocratic quarter. He mended dolls of all sizes and ages, boy dolls and girl dolls, baby dolls in long clothes, and grown-up dolls in fashionable gowns, talking dolls and dumb dolls, those that shut their eyes when they lay down, and those whose eyes had to be shut for them by means of a mysterious wire. His daughter Else was only just over twelve years old, but she was already very clever at mending dolls' clothes, and at doing their hair, which is harder than you might think, though the dolls sit quite still while it is being done.

Mr. Puckler had originally been a German, but he had dissolved his nationality in the ocean of London many years ago, like a great many foreigners. He still had one or two German friends, however, who came on Saturday evenings, and smoked with him and played picquet or "skat" with him for farthing points, and called him "Herr Doctor," which seemed to please Mr. Puckler very much.

He looked older than he was, for his beard was rather long and ragged, his hair was grizzled and thin, and he wore horn-rimmed spectacles. As for Else, she was a thin, pale child, very quiet and neat, with dark eyes and brown hair that was plaited down her back and tied with a bit of black ribbon. She mended the dolls' clothes and took the dolls back to their homes when they were quite strong again.

The house was a little one, but too big for the two people who lived in it. There was a small sitting-room on the street, and the workshop was at the back, and there were three rooms upstairs. But the father and daughter lived most of their time in the workshop, because they were generally at work, even in the evenings.

Mr. Puckler laid Nina on the table and looked at her a long time, till the tears began to fill his eyes behind the horn-rimmed spectacles. He was a very susceptible man, and he often fell in love with the dolls he mended, and found it hard to part with them when they had smiled at him for a few days. They were real little people to him, with characters and thoughts and feelings of their own, and he was very tender with them all. But some attracted him especially from the first, and when they were brought to him maimed and injured, their state seemed so pitiful to him that the tears came easily. You must remember that he had lived among dolls during a great part of his life, and understood them.

"How do you know that they feel nothing?" he went on to say to Else. "You must be gentle with them. It costs nothing to be kind to the little beings, and perhaps it makes a difference to them."

And Else understood him, because she was a child, and she knew that she was more to him than all the dolls.

He fell in love with Nina at first sight, perhaps because her beautiful brown glass eyes were something like Else's own, and he loved Else first and best, with all his heart. And, besides, it was a very sorrowful case. Nina had evidently not been long in the world, for her complexion was perfect, her hair was smooth where it should be smooth, and curly where it should be curly, and her silk clothes were perfectly new. But across her face was that frightful gash, like a sabre-cut, deep and shadowy within, but clean and sharp at the edges. When he tenderly pressed her head to close the gaping wound, the edges made a fine grating sound, that was painful to hear, and the lids of the dark eyes quivered and trembled as though Nina were suffering dreadfully.

109

"Poor Nina!" he exclaimed sorrowfully. "But I shall not hurt you much, though you will take a long time to get strong."

He always asked the names of the broken dolls when they were brought to him, and sometimes the people knew what the children called them, and told him. He liked "Nina" for a name. Altogether and in every way she pleased him more than any doll he had seen for many years, and he felt drawn to her, and made up his mind to make her perfectly strong and sound, no matter how much labour it might cost him.

Mr. Puckler worked patiently a little at a time, and Else watched him. She could do nothing for poor Nina, whose clothes needed no mending. The longer the doll doctor worked, the more fond he became of the yellow hair and the beautiful brown glass eyes. He sometimes forgot all the other dolls that were waiting to be mended, lying side by side on a shelf, while he racked his ingenuity for some new invention by which to hide even the smallest trace of the terrible accident.

She was wonderfully mended. Even he was obliged to admit that; but the scar was still visible to his keen eyes, a very fine line right across the face, downwards from right to left. Yet all the conditions had been most favourable for a cure, since the cement had set quite hard at the first attempt and the weather had been fine and dry, which makes a great difference in a dolls' hospital.

At last he knew that he could do no more, and the under nurse had already come twice to see whether the job was finished, as she coarsely expressed it.

"Nina is not quite strong yet," Mr. Puckler had answered each time, for he could not make up his mind to face the parting.

And now he sat before the square deal table at which he worked, and Nina lay before him for the last time with a big brown paper box beside her. It stood there like her coffin, waiting for her, he thought. He must put her into it, and lay tissue paper over her dear face, and then put on the lid, and at the thought of tying the string his sight was dim with tears again. He was never to look into the glassy depths of the beautiful brown eyes any more, nor to hear the little wooden voice say "Pa-pa" and "Ma-ma." It was a very painful moment.

In the vain hope of gaining time before the separation, he took up the little sticky bottles of cement and glue and gum and colour, looking at each one in turn, and then at Nina's face. And all his small tools lay there, neatly arranged in a row, but he knew that he could not use them again for Nina. She was quite strong at last, and in a country where there should be no cruel children to hurt her she might live a hundred years, with only that almost imperceptible line across her face to tell of the fearful thing that had befallen her on the marble steps of Cranston House.

Suddenly Mr. Puckler's heart was quite full, and he rose abruptly from his seat and turned away.

"Else," he said unsteadily, "you must do it for me. I cannot bear to see her go into the box."

So he went and stood at the window with his back turned, while Else did what he had not the heart to do.

"Is it done?" he asked, not turning around. "Then take her away, my dear. Put on your hat, and take her to Cranston House quickly, and when you are gone I will turn around."

Else was used to her father's queer ways with the dolls, and though she had never seen him so much moved by a parting, she was not much surprised.

"Come back quickly," he said, when he heard her hand on the latch. "It is growing late, and I should not send you at this hour. But I cannot bear to look forward to it any more."

When Else was gone, he left the window and sat down in his place before the table again, to wait for the child to come back. He touched the place where Nina had lain, very gently, and he recalled the softly tinted pink face, and the glass eyes, and the ringlets of yellow hair, till he could almost see them.

The evenings were long, for it was late in the spring. But it began to grow dark soon, and Mr. Puckler wondered why Else did not come back. She had been gone an hour and a half, and that was much longer than he had expected, for it was barely half a mile from Belgrave Square to Cranston House. He reflected that the child might have been kept waiting, but as the twilight deepened he grew anxious, and walked up and down in the dim workshop, no longer thinking of Nina, but of Else, his own living child, whom he loved.

An undefinable, disquieting sensation came upon him by fine degrees, a chilliness and a faint stirring of his thin hair, joined with a wish to be in any company rather than to be alone much longer. It was the beginning of fear.

He told himself in strong German-English that he was a foolish old man, and he began to feel about for the matches in the dusk. He knew just where they should be, for he always kept them in the same place, close to the little tin box that held bits of sealing-wax of various colours, for some kinds of mending. But somehow he could not find the matches in the gloom.

Something had happened to Else, he was sure, and as his fear increased, he felt as though it might be allayed if he could get a light and see what time it was. Then he called himself a foolish old man again, and the sound of his own voice startled him in the dark. He could not find the matches.

The window was grey still; he might see what time it was if he went close to it, and he could go and get

112

matches out of the cupboard afterwards. He stood back from the table, to get out of the way of the chair, and began to cross the board floor.

Something was following him in the dark. There was a small pattering, as of tiny feet upon the boards. He stopped and listened, and the roots of his hair tingled. It was nothing, and he was a foolish old man. He made two steps more, and he was sure that he heard the little pattering again. He turned his back to the window, leaning against the sash so that the panes began to crack, and he faced the dark. Everything was quite still, and it smelt of paste and cement and wood-filings as usual.

"Is that you, Else?" he asked, and he was surprised by the fear in his voice.

There was no answer in the room, and he held up his watch and tried to make out what time it was by the grey dusk that was just not darkness. So far as he could see, it was within two or three minutes of ten o'clock. He had been a long time alone. He was shocked, and frightened for Else, out in London, so late, and he almost ran across the room to the door. As he fumbled for the latch, he distinctly heard the running of the little feet after him.

"Mice!" he exclaimed feebly, just as he got the door open.

He shut it quickly behind him, and felt as though some cold thing had settled on his back and were writhing upon him. The passage was quite dark, but he found his hat and was out in the alley in a moment, breathing more freely, and surprised to find how much light there still was in the open air. He could see the pavement clearly under his feet, and far off in the street to which the alley led he could hear the laughter and calls of children, playing some game out of doors. He wondered how he could have been so nervous, and for an instant he thought of going back into the house to wait quietly for Else. But instantly he felt that nervous fright of something stealing over him again. In any case it was better to walk up to Cranston House and ask the servants about the child. One of the women had perhaps taken a fancy to her, and was even now giving her tea and cake.

He walked quickly to Belgrave Square, and then up the broad streets, listening as he went, whenever there was no other sound, for the tiny footsteps. But he heard nothing, and was laughing at himself when he rang the servants' bell at the big house. Of course, the child must be there.

The person who opened the door was quite an inferior person, for it was a back door, but affected the manners of the front, and stared at Mr. Puckler superciliously under the strong light.

No little girl had been seen, and he knew "nothing about no dolls."

"She is my little girl, said Mr. Puckler tremulously, for all his anxiety was returning tenfold, "and I am afraid something has happened."

The inferior person said rudely that "nothing could have happened to her in that house, because she had not been there, which was a jolly good reason why;" and Mr. Puckler was obliged to admit that the man ought to know, as it was his business to keep the door and let people in. He wished to be allowed to speak to the under nurse, who knew him; but the man was ruder than ever, and finally shut the door in his face.

When the doll doctor was alone in the street, he steadied himself by the railing, for he felt as though he were breaking in two, just as some dolls break, in the middle of the backbone.

Presently he knew that he must be doing something to find Else, and that gave him strength. He began to walk as quickly as he could through the streets, following every highway and byway which his little girl might have taken on her errand. He also asked several policemen in vain if they had seen her, and most of them answered him kindly, for they saw that he was a sober man and in his right senses, and some of them had little girls of their own.

It was one o'clock in the morning when he went up to his own door again, worn out and hopeless and broken-hearted. As he turned the key in the lock, his heart stood still, for he knew that he was awake and not dreaming, and that he really heard those tiny footsteps pattering to meet him inside the house along the passage.

But he was too unhappy to be much frightened any more, and his heart went on again with a dull regular pain, that found its way all through him with every pulse. So he went in, and hung up his hat in the dark, and found the matches in the cupboard and the candlestick in its place in the corner.

Mr. Puckler was so much overcome and so completely worn out that he sat down in his chair before the work-table and almost fainted, as his face dropped forward upon his folded hands. Beside him the solitary candle burned steadily with a low flame in the still warm air.

"Else! Else!" he moaned against his yellow knuckles. And that was all he could say, and it was no relief to him. On the contrary, the very sound of the name was a new and sharp pain that pierced his ears and his head and his very soul. For every time he repeated the name it meant that little Else was dead, somewhere out in the streets of London in the dark.

He was so terribly hurt that he did not even feel something pulling gently at the skirt of his old coat, so gently that it was like the nibbling of a tiny mouse. He might have thought that it was really a mouse if he had noticed it.

"Else! Else!" he groaned right against his hands.

Then a cool breath stirred his thin hair, and the low flame of the one candle dropped down almost to a mere spark, not flickering as though a draught were going to blow it out, but just dropping down as if it were tired out. Mr. Puckler felt his hands stiffening with fright under his face; and there was a faint rustling sound, like some small silk thing blown in a gentle breeze. He sat up straight, stark and scared, and a small wooden voice spoke in the stillness.

"Pa-pa," it said, with a break between the syllables.

Mr. Puckler stood up in a single jump, and his chair fell over backwards with a smashing noise upon the wooden floor. The candle had almost gone out.

It was Nina's doll voice that had spoken, and he should have known it among the voices of a hundred other dolls. And yet there was something more in it, a little human ring, with a pitiful cry and a call for help, and the wail of a hurt child. Mr. Puckler stood up, stark and stiff, and tried to look round, but at first he could not, for he seemed to be frozen from head to foot.

Then he made a great effort, and he raised one hand to each of his temples, and pressed his own head round as he would have turned a doll's. The candle was burning so low that it might as well have been out altogether, for any light it gave, and the room seemed quite dark at first. Then he saw something. He would not have believed that he could be more frightened than he had been just before that. But he was, and his knees shook, for he saw the doll standing in the middle of the floor, shining with a faint and ghostly radiance, her beautiful glassy brown eyes fixed on his. And across her face the very thin line of the break he had mended

116

shone as though it were drawn in light with a fine point of white flame.

Yet there was something more in the eyes, too; there was something human, like Else's own, but as if only the doll saw him through them, and not else. And there was enough of Else to bring back all his pain and to make him forget his fear.

"Else! my little Else!" he cried aloud.

The small ghost moved, and its doll-arm slowly rose and fell with a stiff, mechanical motion.

"Pa-pa," it said.

It seemed this time that there was even more of Else's tone echoing somewhere between the wooden notes that reached his ears so distinctly, and yet so far away. Else was calling him, he was sure.

His face was perfectly white in the gloom, but his knees did not shake any more, and he felt that he was less frightened.

"Yes, child! But where? Where?" he asked. "Where are you, Else?"

"Pa-pa!"

The syllables died away in the quiet room. There was a low rustling of silk, the glassy brown eyes turned slowly away, and Mr. Puckler heard the pitter-patter of the small feet in the bronze kid slippers as the figure ran straight to the door. Then the candle burned high again, the room was full of light, and he was alone.

Mr. Puckler passed his hand over his eyes and looked about him. He could see everything quite clearly, and he felt that he must have been dreaming, though he was standing instead of sitting down, as he should have been if he had just waked up. The candle burned brightly now. There were the dolls to be mended, lying in a row with their toes up. The third one had lost her right shoe, and Else was making one. He knew that, and he was certainly not dreaming now. He had not been dreaming when he had come in from his fruitless search and had heard the doll's footsteps running to the door. He had not fallen asleep in his chair. How could he possibly have fallen asleep when his heart was breaking? He had been awake all the time.

He steadied himself, set the fallen chair upon its legs, and said to himself again very emphatically that he was a foolish old man. He ought to be out in the streets looking for his child, asking questions, and enquiring at the police stations, where all accidents were reported as soon as they were known, or at the hospitals.

"Pa-pa!"

The longing, wailing, pitiful little wooden cry rang from the passage, outside the door, and Mr. Puckler stood for an instant with white face, transfixed and rooted to the spot. A moment later his hand was on the latch. Then he was in the passage, with the light streaming from the open door behind him.

Quite at the other end he saw the little phantom shining clearly in the shadow, and the right hand seemed to beckon to him as the arm rose and fell once more. He knew all at once that it had not come to frighten him but to lead him, and when it disappeared, and he walked boldly towards the door, he knew that it was in the street outside, waiting for him. He forgot that he was tired and had eaten no supper, and had walked many miles, for a sudden hope ran through and through him, like a golden stream of life.

And sure enough, at the corner of the alley, and at the corner of the street, and out in Belgrave Square, he saw the small ghost flitting before him. Sometimes it was only a shadow, where there was other light, but then the glare of the lamps made a pale green sheen on its little Mother Hubbard frock of silk; and sometimes, where the streets were dark and silent, the whole figure shone out brightly, with its yellow curls and rosy neck. It seemed to trot along like a tiny child, and Mr. Puckler could almost hear the pattering of the bronze kid slippers on the pavement as it ran. But it went very fast, and he could only just keep up with it, tearing along with his hat on the back of his head and his thin hair blown by the night breeze, and his horn-rimmed spectacles firmly set upon his broad nose.

On and on he went, and he had no idea where he was. He did not even care, for he knew certainly that he was going the right way.

Then at last, in a wide, quiet street, he was standing before a big, sober-looking door that had two lamps on each side of it, and a polished brass bell-handle, which he pulled.

And just inside, when the door opened, in the bright light, there was the little shadow, and the pale green sheen of the little silk dress, and once more the small cry came to his ears, less pitiful, more longing.

"Pa-pa!"

The shadow turned suddenly bright, and out of the brightness the beautiful brown glass eyes were turned up happily to his, while the rosy mouth smiled so divinely that the phantom doll looked almost like a little angel just then.

"A little girl was brought in soon after ten o'clock," said the quiet voice of the hospital doorkeeper. "I think they thought she was only stunned. She was holding a big brown-paper box against her, and they could not get it out of her arms. She had a long plait of brown hair that hung down as they carried her."

"She is my little girl," said Mr. Puckler, but he hardly heard his own voice.

He leaned over Else's face in the gentle light of the children's ward, and when he had stood there a minute the beautiful brown eyes opened and looked up to his.

119

"Pa-pa!" cried Else, softly, "I knew you would come!"

Then Mr. Puckler did not know what he did or said for a moment, and what he felt was worth all the fear and terror and despair that had almost killed him that night. But by and by Else was telling her story, and the nurse let her speak, for there were only two other children in the room, who were getting well and were sound asleep.

"They were big boys with bad faces," said Else, "and they tried to get Nina away from me, but I held on and fought as well as I could till one of them hit me with something, and I don't remember any more, for I tumbled down, and I suppose the boys ran away, and somebody found me there. But I'm afraid Nina is all smashed."

"Here is the box," said the nurse. "We could not take it out of her arms till she came to herself. Should you like to see if the doll is broken?"

And she undid the string cleverly, but Nina was all smashed to pieces. Only the gentle light of the children's ward made a pale green sheen in the folds of the little Mother Hubbard frock.

THE GRAY CHAMPION

Nathaniel Hawthorne

There was once a time when New England groaned under the actual pressure of heavier wrongs than those threatened ones which brought on the revolution. James II, the bigoted successor of Charles the Voluptuous, had annulled the charters of all the colonies, and sent a harsh and unprincipled soldier to take away our liberties and endanger our religion. The administration of Sir Edmund Andros lacked scarcely a single characteristic of tyranny: a Governor and Council, holding office from the King, and wholly independent of the country; laws made and taxes levied without concurrence of the people immediate or by their representatives; the rights of private citizens violated, and the titles of all landed property declared void; the voice of complaint stifled by restrictions on the press; and, finally, disaffection overawed by the first band of mercenary troops that ever marched on our free soil. For two years our ancestors were kept in sullen submission by that filial love which had invariably secured their allegiance to the mother country, whether its head chanced to be a Parliament, Protector, or Popish Monarch. Till these evil times, however, such allegiance had been merely nominal, and the colonists had ruled themselves, enjoying far more freedom than is even yet the privilege of the native subjects of Great Britain.

At length a rumor reached our shores that the Prince of Orange had ventured on an enterprise, the success of which would be the triumph of civil and religious rights and the salvation of New England. It was but a doubtful whisper; it might be false, or the attempt might fail; and, in either case, the man that stirred against King James would lose his head. Still the intelligence produced a marked effect. The people smiled mysteriously in the streets, and threw bold glances at their oppressors; while, far and wide, there was a subdued and silent agitation, as if the slightest signal would rouse the whole land from its sluggish despondency. Aware of their danger, the rulers resolved to avert it by an imposing display of strength, and perhaps to confirm their despotism by yet harsher measures. One afternoon in April, 1689, Sir Edmund Andros and his favorite councillors, being warm with wine, assembled the redcoats of the Governor's Guard, and made their appearance in the streets of Boston. The sun was near setting when the march commenced.

The roll of the drum, at that unquiet crisis, seemed to go through the streets, less as the martial music of the soldiers, than as a muster-call to the inhabitants themselves. A multitude, by various avenues, assembled in King Street, which was destined to be the scene, nearly a century afterwards, of another encounter between the troops of Britain and a people struggling against her tyranny. Though more than sixty years had elapsed since the Pilgrims came, this crowd of their descendants still showed the strong and sombre features of their character, perhaps more strikingly in such a stern emergency than on happier occasions. There were the sober garb, the general severity of mien, the gloomy but undismayed expression, the Scriptural forms of speech, and the confidence in Heaven's blessing on a righteous cause, which would have marked a band of the original Puritans, when threatened by some peril of the wilderness. Indeed, it was not yet time for the old spirit to be extinct; since there were men in the street, that day, who had worshipped there beneath the trees, before a house was reared to the God for whom they had become exiles. Old soldiers of the Parliament were here, too, smiling grimly at the thought that their aged arms might strike another blow against the house of Stuart. Here, also, were the veterans of King Philip's war, who had burned villages and slaughtered young and old, with pious fierceness, while the godly souls throughout the land were helping them with prayer. Several ministers were scattered among the crowd, which, unlike all other mobs, regarded them with such reverence, as if there were sanctity in their very garments. These holy men exerted their influence to quiet the people, but not to disperse them. Meantime, the purpose of the Governor, in disturbing the peace of the town, at a period when the slightest commotion might throw the country into a ferment, was almost the universal subject of inquiry, and variously explained.

"Satan will strike his master-stroke presently," cried some, "because he knoweth that his time is short. All our godly pastors are to be dragged to prison! We shall see them at a Smithfield fire in King Street!"

Hereupon the people of each parish gathered closer round their minister, who looked calmly upwards and assumed a more apostolic dignity, as well befitted a candidate for the highest honor of his profession, the crown of martyrdom. It was actually fancied, at that period, that New England might have a John Rogers of her own, to take the place of that worthy in the Primer.

"The Pope of Rome has given orders for a new St. Bartholomew!" cried others. "We are to be massacred, man and male child!"

Neither was this rumor wholly discredited, although the wiser class believed the Governor's object somewhat less atrocious. His predecessor under the old charter, Bradstreet, a venerable companion of the first settlers, was known to be in town. There were grounds for conjecturing that Sir Edmund Andros intended, at once, to strike terror, by a parade of military force, and to confound the opposite faction by possessing himself of their chief.

"Stand firm for the old charter, Governor!" shouted the crowd, seizing upon the idea. "The good old Governor Bradstreet!"

While this cry was at the loudest, the people were surprised by the well-known figure of Governor Bradstreet himself, a patriarch of nearly ninety, who appeared on the elevated steps of a door, and, with characteristic mildness, besought them to submit to the constituted authorities.

"My children," concluded this venerable person, "do nothing rashly. Cry not aloud, but pray for the welfare of New England, and expect patiently what the Lord will do in this matter!"

The event was soon to be decided. All this time, the roll of the drum had been approaching through Cornhill, louder and deeper, till with reverberations from house to house, and the regular tramp of martial footsteps, it burst into the street. A double rank of soldiers made their appearance, occupying the whole breadth of the passage, with shouldered matchlocks, and matches burning, so as to present a row of fires in the dusk.

Their steady march was like the progress of a machine, that would roll irresistibly over everything in its way. Next, moving slowly, with a confused clatter of hoofs on the pavement, rode a party of mounted gentlemen, the central figure being Sir Edmund Andros, elderly, but erect and soldier-like. Those around him were his favorite councillors, and the bitterest foes of New England. At his right hand rode Edward Randolph, our arch-enemy, that "blasted wretch," as Cotton Mather calls him, who achieved the downfall of our ancient government, and was followed with a sensible curse, through life and to his grave. On the other side was Bullivant, scattering jests and mockery as he rode along. Dudley came behind, with a downcast look, dreading, as well he might, to meet the indignant gaze of the people, who beheld him, their only countryman by birth, among the oppressors of his native land. The captain of a frigate in the harbor, and two or three civil officers under the Crown, were also there. But the figure which most attracted the public eye, and stirred up the deepest feeling, was the Episcopal clergyman of King's Chapel, riding haughtily among the magistrates in his priestly vestments, the fitting representative of prelacy and persecution, the union of Church and State, and all those abominations which had driven the Puritans to the wilderness. Another guard of soldiers, in double rank, brought up the rear.

The whole scene was a picture of the condition of New England, and its moral, the deformity of any government that does not grow out of the nature of things and the character of the people. On one side the religious multitude, with their sad visages and dark attire, and on the other, the group of despotic rulers, with the High-Churchman in the midst, and here and there a crucifix at their bosoms, all magnificently clad, flushed with wine, proud of unjust authority, and scoffing at the universal groan. And the mercenary soldiers, waiting but the word to deluge the street with blood, showed the only means by which obedience could be secured.

"O Lord of Hosts," cried a voice among the crowd, "provide a Champion for thy people!"

This ejaculation was loudly uttered, and served as a herald's cry, to introduce a remarkable personage. The crowd had rolled back, and were now huddled together nearly at the extremity of the street, while the soldiers had advanced no more than a third of its length. The intervening space was empty—a paved solitude, between lofty edifices, which threw almost a twilight shadow over it. Suddenly, there was seen the figure of an ancient man, who seemed to have emerged from among the people, and was walking by himself along the centre of the street, to confront the armed band. He wore the old Puritan dress, a dark cloak and a steeple-crowned hat, in the fashion of at least fifty years before, with a heavy sword upon his thigh, but a staff in his hand to assist the tremulous gait of age.

When at some distance from the multitude, the old man turned slowly round, displaying a face of antique majesty, rendered doubly venerable by the hoary beard that descended on his breast. He made a gesture at once of encouragement and warning, then turned again, and resumed his way.

"Who is this gray patriarch?" asked the young men of their sires.

"Who is this venerable brother?" asked the old men among themselves.

But none could make reply. The fathers of the people, those of fourscore years and upwards, were disturbed, deeming it strange that they should forget one of such evident authority, whom they must have known in their early days, the associate of Winthrop, and all the old councillors, giving laws, and making prayers, and leading them against the savage. The elderly men ought to have remembered him, too, with locks as gray in their youth as their own were now. And the young! How could he have passed so utterly from their memories— that hoary site, the relic of long-departed times, whose awful benediction had surely been bestowed on their uncovered heads, in childhood?

"Whence did he come? What is his purpose? Who can this old man be?" whispered the wondering crowd.

Meanwhile, the venerable stranger, staff in hand, was pursuing his solitary walk along the centre of the street. As he drew near the advancing soldiers, and as the roll of their drum came full upon his ear, the old man raised himself to a loftier mien, while the decrepitude of age seemed to fall from his shoulders, leaving him in gray but unbroken dignity. Now, he marched onward with a warrior's step, keeping time to the military music. Thus the aged form advanced on one side, and the whole parade of soldiers and magistrates on the other, till, when scarcely twenty yards remained between, the old grasped his staff by the middle, and held it before him like a leader's truncheon.

"Stand!" cried he.

The eye, the face, the attitude of command; the solemn, yet warlike peal of that voice, fit either to rule a host in the battlefield or be raised to God in prayer, were irresistible. At the old man's word and outstretched arm, the roll of the drum was hushed at once, and the advancing line stood still. A tremulous enthusiasm seized upon the multitude. That stately form, combining the leader and the saint, so gray, so dimly seen in such an ancient garb, could only belong to some old champion of the righteous cause, whom the oppressor's drum had summoned from his grave. They raised a shout of awe and exultation, and looked for the deliverance of New England.

BODIES OF THE DEAD

The Governor, and the gentlemen of his party, perceiving themselves brought to an unexpected stand, rode hastily forward, as if they would have pressed their snorting and affrighted horses right against the hoary apparition. He, however, blenched not a step, but glancing his severe eye round the group, which half encompassed him, at last bent it sternly on Sir Edmund Andros. One would have thought that the dark old man was chief ruler there, and that the Governor and Council, with soldiers at their back, representing the whole power and authority of the Crown, had no alternative but obedience.

"What does this old fellow here?" cried Edward Randolph, fiercely. "On, Sir Edmund! Bid the soldiers forward, and give the dotard the same choice that you give all his countrymen—to stand aside or be trampled on!"

"Nay, nay, let us show respect to the good grandsire," said Bullivant, laughing. "See you not, he is some old round-headed dignitary, who hath lain asleep these thirty years, and knows nothing of the change of times? Doubtless, he thinks to put us down with a proclamation in Old Noll's name!"

"Are you mad, old man?" demanded Sir Edmund Andros, in loud and harsh tones. "How dare you stay the march of King James's Governor?"

"I have stayed the march of a king himself, ere now," replied the gray figure, with stern composure. "I am here, Sir Governor, because the cry of an oppressed people hath disturbed me in my secret place; and beseeching this favor earnestly of the Lord, it was vouchsafed me to appear once again on earth, in the good old cause of his saints. And what speak ye of James? There is no longer a Popish tyrant on the throne of England, and by tomorrow noon his name shall be a byword in this very street, where ye would make it a word of terror. Back, thou that wast a Governor, back! With this night thy power is ended,—tomorrow, the prison!—back, lest I foretell the scaffold!"

The people had been drawing nearer and nearer, and drinking in the words of their champion, who spoke in accents long disused, like one unaccustomed to converse, except with the dead of many years ago. But his voice stirred their souls. They confronted the soldiers, not wholly without arms, and ready to convert the very stones of the street into deadly weapons. Sir Edmund Andros looked at the old man; then he cast his hard and cruel eye over the multitude, and beheld them burning with that lurid wrath, so difficult to kindle or to quench; and again he fixed his gaze on the aged form, which stood obscurely in an open space, where neither friend nor foe had thrust himself. What were his thoughts, he uttered no word which might discover. But whether the oppressor were overawed by the Gray Champion's look, or perceived his peril in the threatening attitude of the people, it is certain that he gave back, and ordered his soldiers to commence a slow and guarded retreat. Before another sunset, the Governor, and all that rode so proudly with him, were prisoners, and long ere it was known that James had abdicated, King William was proclaimed throughout New England.

But where was the Gray Champion? Some reported that, when the troops had gone from King Street, and the people were thronging tumultuously in their rear, Bradstreet, the aged Governor, was seen to embrace a form more aged than his own. Others soberly affirmed that, while they marvelled at the venerable grandeur of his aspect, the old man had faded from their eyes, melting slowly into the hues of twilight, till, where he stood, there was an empty space. But all agreed that the hoary shape was gone. The men of that generation watched for his reappearance, in sunshine and in twilight, but never saw him more, nor knew when his funeral passed, nor where his gravestone was.

And who was the Gray Champion? Perhaps his name might be found in the records of that stern Court of Justice, which passed a sentence, too mighty for the age, but glorious in all after times, for its humbling lesson to the monarch and its high example to the subject. I have heard that, whenever the descendants of the Puritans are to show the spirit of their sires, the old man appears again. When eighty years had passed, he walked once more in King Street. Five years later, in the twilight of an April morning, he stood on the green, beside the meeting-house, at Lexington, where now the obelisk of granite, with a slab of slate inlaid, commemorates the first fallen of the Revolution. And when our fathers were toiling at the breastwork on Bunker's Hill, all through that night the old warrior walked his rounds. Long, long may it be, ere he comes again! His hour is one of darkness, and adversity, and peril. But should domestic tyranny oppress us, or the invader's step pollute our soil, still may the Gray Champion come, for he is the type of New England's hereditary spirit, and his shadowy march, on the eve of danger, must ever be the pledge that New England's sons will vindicate their ancestry.

THE BOY WHO DREW CATS

Lafcadio Hearn

A long, long time ago, in a small country village in Japan, there lived a poor farmer and his wife, who were very good people. They had a number of children, and found it hard to feed them all. The elder son was strong enough when only fourteen years old to help his father; and the little girls learned to help their mother almost as soon as they could walk.

But the youngest child, a little boy, did not seem to be fit for hard work. He was very clever—cleverer than all his brothers and sisters; but he was quite weak and small, and people said he could never grow very big. So his parents thought it would be better for him to become a priest than to become a farmer. They took him with them to the village temple one day, and asked the good old priest who lived there if he would have their little boy for his pupil, and teach him all that a priest ought to know.

The old man spoke kindly to the lad, and asked

him some hard questions. So clever were the answers that the priest agreed to take the little fellow into the temple as an acolyte, and to educate him for the priesthood.

The boy learned quickly what the old priest taught him, and was very obedient in most things. But he had one fault. He liked to draw cats during study-hours, and to draw cats when cats ought not to have been drawn at all.

Whenever he found himself alone, he drew cats. He drew them on the margins of the priest's books, and on all the screens of the temple, on the walls, and on the pillars. Several times the priest told him this was not right; but he did not stop drawing cats. He drew them because he could not really help it. He had what is called "the genius of an artist," and just for that reason he was not quite fit to be an acolyte; a good acolyte should study books.

One day after he had drawn some very clever pictures of cats upon a paper screen, the old priest said to him severely, "My boy, you must go away from this temple at once. You will never make a good priest, but perhaps you will become a great artist. Now let me give you a last piece of advice, and be sure you never forget it. *Avoid large places at night; keep to small!*"

The boy did not know what the priest meant by saying, *"Avoid large places; keep to small!"* He thought and thought, while he was tying up his little bundle of clothes to go away; but he could not understand those words, and he was afraid to speak to the priest any more, except to say good-bye

He left the temple very sorrowfully, and began to wonder what he should do. If he went straight home he felt his father would punish him for having been disobedient to the priest: so he was afraid to go home. All at once he remembered that at the next village, twelve miles away, there was a very big temple. He had heard there were several priests at that temple; and he made up his mind to go to them and ask them to take him for their acolyte.

Now that big temple was closed up but the boy did not know this fact. The reason it had been closed up was that a goblin had frightened the priests away, and had taken possession of the place. Some brave warriors had afterwards gone to the temple at night to kill the goblin; but they had never been seen alive again. Nobody had ever told these things to the boy; so he walked all the way to the village hoping to be kindly treated by the priests.

When he got to the village it was already dark, and all the people were in bed; but he saw the big temple on a hill on the other end of the principal street, and he saw there was a light in the temple. People who tell the story say the goblins used to make that light, in order to tempt lonely travellers to ask for shelter. The boy went at once to the temple, and knocked. There was no sound inside. He knocked and knocked again; but still nobody came. At last he pushed gently at the door, and was glad to find that it had not been fastened. So he went in and saw a lamp burning—but no priest.

He thought that some priest would be sure to come very soon, and he sat down and waited. Then he noticed that everything in the temple was gray with dust, and thickly spun over with cobwebs. So he thought to himself that the priests would certainly like to have an acolyte, to keep the place clean. He wondered why they had allowed the place to get so dusty. What most pleased him, however, were some big white screens, good to paint cats upon. Though he was tired, he looked

133

at once for a writing box and found one, and ground some ink, and began to paint cats.

He painted a great many cats upon the screens; and then he began to feel very, very sleepy. He was just on the point of lying down to sleep beside one of the screens, when he suddenly remembered the words: *"Avoid large places—keep to small!"*

The temple was very large; he was alone; and as he thought of these words—though he could not quite understand them—he began to feel for the first time a little afraid; and he resolved to look for a small place in which to sleep. He found a little cabinet, with a sliding door, and went into it and shut himself up. Then he lay down and fell fast asleep.

Very late in the night he was awakened by a most terrible noise—a noise of fighting and screaming. It was so dreadful that he was afraid even to look through a chink of the little cabinet; he lay very still, holding his breath for fright.

The light that had been in the temple went out; but the awful sounds continued, and became more awful, and all the temple shook. After a long time silence came; but the boy was still afraid to move. He did not move until the light of the morning sun shone into the cabinet through the chinks of the little door.

Then he got out of his hiding-place very cautiously, and looked about. The first thing he saw was that all the floor of the temple was covered with blood. And then he saw, lying dead in the middle of it, an enormous monstrous rat—a goblin-rat—bigger than a cow!

But who or what could have killed it? There was no man or other creature to be seen. Suddenly the boy observed that the mouths of all the cats he had drawn the night before were red and wet with blood. Then he knew that the goblin had been killed by the cats which

he had drawn. And then also, for the first time, he understood why the wise old priest had said to him:—
"Avoid large places at night; keep to small."

Afterwards that boy became a very famous artist. Some of the cats which he drew are still shown to travellers in Japan.

THE SCARECROW

G. Ranger Wormser

B^{en—"}
The woman stood in the doorway of the ramshackle, tumble-down shanty. Her hands were cupped at her mouth. The wind blew loose, whitish blond wisps of hair around her face and slashed the faded blue dress into the uncorseted bulk of her body.

"Benny—oh, Benny—"

Her call echoed through the still evening.

Her eyes staring straight before her down the slope in front of the house caught sight of something blue and antiquatedly military standing waist deep and rigid in the corn field.

"That ole scarecrow," she muttered to herself, "that there old scarecrow with that there ole uniform onto him, too!"

The sun was going slowly just beyond the farthest hill. The unreal light of the skies' reflected colors held over the yellow, waving tips of the corn field.

136

"Benny—," she called again. "Oh—Benny!"

And then she saw him coming toward her, trudging up the hill.

She waited until he stood in front of her.

"Supper, Ben," she said. "Was you down in the south meadow where you couldn't hear me call?"

"Naw."

He was young and slight. He had thick hair and a thin face. His features were small. There was nothing unusual about them. His eyes were deep-set and long, with lids that were heavily fringed.

"You heard me calling you?"

"Yes, maw."

He stood there straight and still. His eyelids were lowered.

"Why ain't you come along then? What ails you, Benny, letting me shout and shout that way?"

"Nothing—maw."

"Where was you?"

He hesitated a second before answering her.

"I was to the bottom of the hill."

"And what was you doing down there to the bottom of the hill? What was you doing down there, Benny?"

Her voice had a hushed tenseness to it.

"I was watching, maw."

"Watching, Benny?"

"That's what I was doing."

His tone held a guarded sullenness.

" 'Tain't no such a pretty sunset, Benny."

"Warn't watching no sunset."

"Benny—!"

"Well." He spoke quickly. "What d'you want to put it there for? What d'you want to do that for in the first place?"

"There was birds, Benny. You know there was birds."

"That ain't what I mean. What for d'you put on that there uniform?"

"I ain't had nothing else. There warn't nothing but your grand-dad's ole uniform. It's fair in rags, Benny. It's all I had to put on to it."

"Well, you done it yourself."

"Naw, Benny, naw! 'Tain't nothing but an ole uniform with a stick into it. Just to frighten off them birds. 'Tain't nothing else. Honest, 'tain't, Benny."

He looked up at her out of the corners of his eyes.

"It was waving its arms."

"That's the wind."

"Naw, maw. Waving its arms before the wind it come up."

"Sush, Benny! 'Tain't likely. 'Tain't."

"I was watching, maw. I seen it wave and wave. S'pose it should beckon— s'pose it should beckon to me. I'd be going, then, maw."

"Sush, Benny."

"I'd fair have to go, maw."

"Leave your mammy? Naw, Ben; naw. You couldn't never go off and leave your mammy. Even if you ain't able to bear this here farm you couldn't go off from your mammy. You couldn't! Not—your—maw—Benny!"

She could see his mouth twitch. She saw him catch his lower lip in under his teeth.

"Aw—"

"Say you couldn't leave, Benny; say it!"

"I—I fair hate this here farm!" He mumbled. "Morning and night—and morning and night. Nothing but chores and earth. And then some more of them chores. And always that there way. So it is! Always! And the stillness! Nothing alive, nothing! Sometimes I ain't able to stand it nohow. Sometimes—!"

"You'll get to like it— later, mebbe—"

"Naw! naw, maw!"

"You will, Benny. Sure you will."

"I won't never. I ain't able to help fretting. It's all closed up tight inside of me. Eating and eating. It makes me feel sick."

She put out a hand and laid it heavily on his shoulder.

"Likely it's a touch of fever in the blood, Benny."

"Aw—! I ain't got no fever!"

"You'll be feeling better in the morning, Ben."

"I'll be feeling the same, maw. That's just it. Always the same. Nothing but the stillness. Nothing alive. And down there in the corn field—"

"That ain't alive, Benny!"

"Ain't it, maw?"

"Don't say that, Benny. Don't!"

He shook her hand off of him.

"I was watching," he said doggedly. "I seen it wave and wave."

She turned into the house.

"That ole scarecrow!" She muttered to herself. "That there ole scarecrow!"

She led the way into the kitchen. The boy followed at her heels.

A lamp was lighted on the center table. The one window was uncurtained. Through the naked spot of it the evening glow poured shimmeringly into the room.

Inside the doorway they both paused.

"You set down, Benny."

He pulled a chair up to the table.

She took a steaming pot from the stove and emptying it into a plate, placed the dish before him.

He fell to eating silently.

She came and sat opposite him. She watched him cautiously. She did not want him to know that she was watching him. Whenever he glanced up she hurried her eyes away from his face. In the stillness the only live

139

things were those two pair of eyes darting away from each other.

"Benny—!" She could not stand it any longer. "Benny—just—you—just—you—"

He gulped down a mouthful of food.

"Aw, maw—don't you start nothing. Not no more tonight, maw."

She half rose from her chair. For a second she leaned stiffly against the table. Then she slipped back into her seat, her whole body limp and relaxed.

"I ain't going to start nothing, Benny. I ain't even going to talk about this here farm. Honest—I ain't."

"Aw—this—here—farm—!"

"I've gave the best years of my life to it."

She spoke the words defiantly.

"You said that all afore, maw."

"It's true," she murmured. "Terrible true. And I done it for you, Benny. I wanted to be giving you something. It's all I'd got to give you, Benny. There's many a man, Ben, that's glad of his farm. And grateful, too. There's many that makes it pay."

"And what'll I do if it does pay, maw? What'll I do then?"

"I—I—don't know, Benny. It's only just beginning, now."

"But if it does pay, maw? What'll I do? Go away from here?"

"Naw, Benny—. Not—away—. What'd you go away for, when it pays? After all them years I gave to it?"

His spoon clattered noisily to his plate. He pushed his chair back from the table. The legs of it rasped loudly along the uncarpeted floor. He got to his feet.

"Let's go on outside," he said. "There ain't no sense to this here talking—and talking."

She glanced up at him. Her eyes were narrow and hard.

"All right, Benny. I'll clear up. I'll be along in a minute. All right, Benny."

He slouched heavily out of the room.

She sat where she was, the set look pressed on her face. Automatically her hands reached out among the dishes, pulling them toward her.

Outside the boy sank down on the step.

It was getting dark. There were shadows along the ground. Blue shadows. In the graying skies one star shone brilliantly. Beyond the mist-slurred summit of a hill the full moon grew yellow.

In front of him was the slope of wind-moved corn field, and in the center of it the dim, military figure standing waist deep in the corn.

His eyes fixed themselves to it.

"Ole—uniform—with—a—stick—into—it."

He whispered the words very low.

Still—standing there—still. The same wooden attitude of it. His same, cunning watching of it.

There was a wind. He knew it was going over his face. He could feel the cool of the wind across his moistened lips.

He took a deep breath.

Down there in the shivering corn field, standing in the dark, blue shadows, the dim figure had quivered.

An arm moved—swaying to and fro. The other arm began—swaying—saying. A tremor ran through it. Once it pivoted. The head shook slowly from side to side. The arms rose and fell—and rose again. The head came up and down and rocked a bit to either side.

"I'm here—" he muttered involuntarily. "Here."

The arms were tossing and stretching.

He thought the head faced in his direction.

The wind had died out.

The arms went down and came up and reached.

"Benny—"

141

The woman seated herself on the step at his side.

"Look!" He mumbled. "Look!"

He pointed his hand at the dim figure shifting restlessly in the quiet, shadow-saturated corn field.

Her eyes followed after his.

"Oh—Benny—"

"Well—" His voice was hoarse. "It's moving, ain't it? You can see it moving for yourself, can't you? You ain't able to say you don't see it, are you?"

"The—wind—" She stammered.

"Where's the wind?"

"Down—there."

"D'you feel a wind? Say, d'you feel a wind?"

"Mebbe—down—there."

"There ain't no wind. Not now—there ain't! And it's moving, ain't it? Say, it's moving, ain't it?"

"It looks like it was dancing. So it does. Like as if it was—making—itself—dance—"

His eyes were still riveted on those arms that came up and down— up and down— and reached.

"It'll stop soon—now." He stuttered it more to himself than to her. "Then—it'll be still. I've watched it mighty often. Mebbe it knows I watch it. Mebbe that's why—it—moves—"

"Aw—Benny—"

"Well, you see it, don't you? You thought there was something the matter with me when I come and told you how it waves—and waves. But you seen it waving, ain't you?"

"It's nothing, Ben. Look, Benny. It's stopped!"

The two of them stared down the slope at the dim, military figure standing rigid and waist deep in the corn field.

The woman gave a quick sigh of relief.

For several moments they were silent.

From somewhere in the distance came the harsh, discordant sound of bull frogs croaking. Out in the night a dog bayed at the golden, full moon climbing up over the hills. A bird circled between sky and earth hovering above the corn field. They saw its slow descent, and then for a second they caught the startled whir of its wings, as it flew blindly into the night.

"That ole scarecrow!" She muttered.

"S'pose—" He whispered. "S'pose when it starts its moving like that;—s'pose some day it walks out of that there corn field! Just naturally walks out here to me. What then, if it walks out?"

"Benny—!"

"That's what I'm thinking of all the time. If it takes it into its head to just naturally walk out here. What's going to stop it, if it wants to walk out after me; once it starts moving that way? What?"

"Benny—! It couldn't do that! It couldn't!"

"Mebbe it won't. Mebbe it'll just beckon first. Mebbe it won't come after me. Not if I go when it beckons. I kind of figure it'll beckon when it wants me. I couldn't stand the other. I couldn't wait for it to come out here after me. I kind of feel it'll beckon. When it beckons, I'll be going."

"Benny, there's sickness coming on you."

" 'Tain't no sickness."

The woman's hands were clinched together in her lap.

"I wish to Gawd—" she said—"I wish I ain't never seen the day when I put that there thing up in that there corn field. But I ain't thought nothing like this could never happen. I wish to Gawd I ain't never seen the day—"

" 'Tain't got nothing to do with you."

His voice was very low.

"It's got everything to do with me. So it has! You said that afore yourself; and you was right. Ain't I put

143

it up? Ain't I looked high and low the house through? Ain't that ole uniform of your grand-dad's been the only rag I could lay my hands on? Was there anything else I could use? Was there?"

"Aw—maw—!"

"Ain't we needed a scarecrow down there? With them birds so awful bad? Pecking away at the corn; and pecking."

" 'Tain't your fault, maw."

"There warn't nothing else but that there ole uniform. I wouldn't have took it, otherwise. Poor ole Pa so desperate proud of it as he was. Him fighting for his country in it. Always saying that he was. He couldn't be doing enough for his country. And that there ole uniform meaning so much to him. Like a part of him I used to think it—and—. You wanting to say something, Ben?"

"Naw—naw—!"

"He wouldn't even let us be burying him in it. 'Put my country's flag next my skin'; he told us. 'When I die keep the ole uniform.' Just like a part of him, he thought it. Wouldn't I have kept it, falling to pieces as it is, if there'd have been anything else to put up there in that there corn field?"

She felt the boy stiffen suddenly.

"And with him a soldier—"

He broke off abruptly.

She sensed what he was about to say.

"Aw, Benny—. That was different. Honest, it was. He warn't the only one in his family. There was two brothers."

The boy got to his feet.

"Why won't you let me go?" He asked it passionately. "Why d'you keep me here? You know I ain't happy! You know all the men've gone from these here parts. You know I ain't happy! Ain't you going to see how much I want to go? Ain't you able to know that I want to fight for my country? The way he did his fighting?"

The boy jerked his head in the direction of the figure standing waist deep in the corn field; standing rigidly and faintly outlined beneath the haunting flood of moonlight.

"Naw, Benny. You can't go. Naw—!"

"Why, maw? Why d'you keep saying that and saying it?"

"I'm all alone, Benny. I've gave all my best years to make the farm pay for you. You got to stay, Benny. You got to stay on here with me. You just plain got—to! You'll be glad some day, Benny. Later—on. You'll be right glad."

She saw him thrust his hands hastily into his trouser pockets.

"Glad?" His voice sounded tired. "I'll be shamed. That's what I'll be. Nothing, d' you hear, nothing—but shamed!"

She started to her feet.

"Benny—" A note of fear shook through the words. "You wouldn't—wouldn't—go?"

He waited a moment before he answered her.

"If you ain't wanting me to go—; I'll stay. Gawd! I guess I plain got to—stay."

"That's a good boy, Benny. You won't never be sorry—nohow—I promise you!—I'll be making it up to you. Honest, I will!—There's lots of ways—I'll—!"

He interrupted her.

"Only, maw—; I won't let it come after me. If it beckons I—got—to—go!"

She gave a sudden laugh that trailed off uncertainly.

" 'Tain't going to beckon, Benny."

"If it beckons, maw—"

" 'Tain't going to, Benny. 'Tain't nothing but the

145

wind that moves it. It's just the wind, sure. Mebbe you got a touch of fever. Mebbe you better go on to bed. You'll be all right in the morning. Just you wait and see. You're a good boy, Benny. You'll never go off and leave your maw and the farm. You're a fine lad, Benny."

"If—it—beckons—" He repeated in weary monotone.

" 'Tain't, Benny!"

"I'll be going to bed," he said.

"That's it, Benny. Good night."

"Good night, maw."

She stood there listening to his feet thudding up the stairs. She heard him knocking about in the room overhead. A door banged. She stood quite still. There were footsteps moving slowly. A window was thrown open.

She looked up to see him leaning far out over the sill.

Her eyes went down the slope of the moonlight-bathed corn field.

Her right hand curled itself into a fist.

"Ole—scarecrow—!"

She half laughed.

She waited there until she saw the boy draw away from the window. She went into the house and bolted the door behind her. Then she went up the narrow steps.

That night she lay awake for a long time. The heat had grown intense. She found herself tossing from side to side of the small bed.

The window shade had stuck at the top of the window.

The moonlight trickled into the room. She could see the window-framed, star-specked patch of the skies. When she sat up she saw the round, reddish-yellow ball of the moon.

She must have dozed, because she woke with a start.

She felt that she had had a fearful, evil dream. The horror of it clung to her.

The room was like an oven.

She thought the walls were coming together and the ceiling pressing down.

Her body was covered with sweat.

She forced herself wide awake. She made herself get out of the bed. She stood for a second uncertain. Then she went to the window.

Not a breath of air stirring.

The moon was high in the sky.

She looked out across the hills.

Down there to the left the acres of potatoes. Potatoes were paying. She counted on a big harvest. To the right the wheat. Only the second year for those five fields. She knew that she had done well with them.

She thought, with a smile running over her lips, back to the time when less than half of the place had been under cultivation. She remembered her dream of getting the whole of her farm in work. She and the boy had made good. She thought of that with savage complacency. It had been a struggle; a bitter, hard fight from the beginning. But she had made good with her farm.

And there down the slope, just in front of the house, the corn field. And in the center of it, standing waist deep in the corn, the antiquated, military figure.

The smile slid from her mouth.

The suffocating heat was terrific.

Not a breath of air.

Suddenly she began to shake from head to foot.

Her eyes wide and staring, were fixed on the moonlight-whitened corn field; her eyes were held to the moonlight-streaked figure standing in the ghostly corn.

Moving—

An arm swayed—swayed to and fro. Backwards and

147

forwards—backwards— The other arm—swaying—A tremor ran through it. Once it pivoted. The head shook slowly from side to side. The arms rose and fell— and rose again. The head came up and down, and rocked a bit to either side.

"Dancing—" She whispered stupidly. "Dancing—"

She thought she could not breathe.

She had never felt such oppressive heat.

The arms were tossing and stretching.

She could not take her eyes from it.

And then she saw both arms reach out, and slowly, very slowly, she saw the hands of them, beckoning.

In the stillness of the room next to her she thought she heard a crash.

She listened intently, her eyes stuck to those reaching arms, and the hands of them that beckoned and beckoned.

"Benny—" She murmured—"Benny—!"

Silence.

She could not think.

It was his talk that had done this—Benny's talk—He had said something about it—walking out—If it should come—out—! Moving all over like that—If its feet should start—! If they should of a sudden begin to shuffle— shuffle out of the cornfield—!

But Benny wasn't awake. He—couldn't—see—it. Thank Gawd! If only something—would—hold—it! If—only—it—would—stop— Gawd!

Nothing stirring out there in the haunting moon-lighted night. Nothing moving. Nothing but the figure standing waist deep in the corn field. And even as she looked, the rigid, military figure grew still. Still, now, but for those slow, beckoning hands.

A tremendous dizziness came over her.

She closed her eyes for a second and then she stumbled back to the bed.

She lay there panting. She pulled the sheets up across her face; her shaking fingers working the tops of them into a hard ball. She stuffed it between her chattering teeth.

Whatever happened, Benny mustn't hear her. She mustn't waken, Benny. Thank Heaven, Benny was asleep. Benny must never know how, out there in the whitened night, the hands of the figure slowly and unceasingly beckoned and beckoned.

The sight of those reaching arms stayed before her. When, hours later, she fell asleep, she still saw the slow-moving, motioning hands.

It was morning when she wakened.

The sun streamed into the room.

She went to the door and opened it.

"Benny—" She called. "Oh, Benny."

There was no answer.

"Benny—" She called again. "Get on up. It's late, Benny!"

The house was quiet.

She half dressed herself and went into his room.

The bed had been slept in. She saw that at a glance. His clothes were not there. Down—in—the—field—because—she'd—forgotten—to—wake—him—.

In a sudden stunning flash she remembered the crash she had heard.

It took her a long while to get to the little closet behind the bed. Before she opened it she knew it would be empty.

The door creaked open.

His one hat and coat were gone.

She had known that.

He had seen those two reaching arms! He had seen those two hands that had slowly, very slowly, beckoned!

She went to the window.

Her eyes staring straight before her, down the slope

in front of the house, caught sight of something blue and antiquatedly military standing waist deep and rigid in the corn field.

"You ole scarecrow—!" She whimpered. "Why're you standing there?" She sobbed. "What're you standing still for—*now*?"

CIRCUMSTANCE

Harriet Prescott Spofford

S he had remained, during all that day, with a sick
neighbor,—those eastern wilds of Maine in that
epoch frequently making neighbors and miles
synonymous,—and so busy had she been with care and
sympathy that she did not at first observe the approaching night. But finally the level rays, reddening the snow,
threw their gleam upon the wall, and, hastily donning
cloak and hood, she bade her friends farewell and sal-
lied forth on her return. Home lay some three miles
distant, across a copse, a meadow, and a piece of
woods,—the woods being a fringe on the skirts of the
great forests that stretch far away into the North. That
home was one of a dozen log-houses lying a few fur-
longs apart from each other, with their half-cleared de-
mesnes separating them at the rear from a wilderness
untrodden save by stealthy native or deadly panther
tribes.

She was in a nowise exalted frame of spirit,—on the

contrary, rather depressed by the pain she had witnessed and the fatigue she had endured; but in certain temperaments such a condition throws open the mental pores, so to speak, and renders one receptive of every influence. Through the little copse she walked slowly, with her cloak folded about her, lingering to imbibe the sense of shelter, the sunset filtered in purple through the mist of woven spray and twig, the companionship of growth not sufficiently dense to band against her, the sweet homefeeling of a young and tender wintry wood. It was therefore just on the edge of the evening that she emerged from the place and began to cross the meadowland. At one hand lay the forest to which her path wound; at the other the evening star hung over a tide of failing orange that slowly slipped down the earth's broad side to sadden other hemispheres with sweet regret. Walking rapidly now, and with her eyes wide-open, she distinctly saw in the air before her what was not there a moment ago, a winding-sheet,—cold, white, and ghastly, waved by the likeness of four wan hands,—that rose with a long inflation, and fell in rigid folds, while a voice, shaping itself from the hollowness above, spectral and melancholy, sighed,—"The Lord have mercy on the people! The Lord have mercy on the people!" Three times the sheet with its corpse-covering outline waved beneath the pale hands, and the voice, awful in its solemn and mysterious depth, sighed, "The Lord have mercy on the people!" Then all was gone, the place was clear again, the gray sky was obstructed by no deathly blot; she looked about her, shook her shoulders decidedly, and, pulling on her hood, went forward once more.

She might have been a little frightened by such an apparition, if she had led a life of less reality than frontier settlers are apt to lead; but dealing with hard fact does not engender a flimsy habit of mind, and this

woman was too sincere and earnest in her character, and
too happy in her situation, to be thrown by antagonism,
merely, upon superstitious fancies and chimeras of the
second-sight. She did not even believe herself subject to
an hallucination, but smiled simply, a little vexed that
her thought could have framed such a glamour from the
day's occurrences, and not sorry to lift the bough of the
warder of the woods and enter and disappear in their
sombre path. If she had been imaginative, she would
have hesitated at her first step into a region whose dangers were not visionary; but I suppose that the thought
of a little child at home would conquer that propensity
in the most habituated. So, biting a bit of spicy birch,
she went along. Now and then she came to a gap where
the trees had been partially felled, and here she found
that the lingering twilight was explained by that peculiar and perhaps electric film which sometimes sheathes
the sky in diffused light for many hours before a brilliant aurora. Suddenly, a swift shadow, like the fabulous
flying-dragon, writhed through the air before her, and
she felt herself instantly seized and borne aloft. It was
that wild beast—the most savage and serpentine and
subtle and fearless of our latitudes—known by hunters
as the Indian Devil, and he held her in his clutches on
the broad floor of a swinging fir-bough. His long sharp
claws were caught in her clothing, he worried them sa-
gaciously a little, then, finding that ineffectual to free
them, he commenced licking her bare arm with his
rasping tongue and pouring over her the wide streams
of his hot, fetid breath. So quick had this flashing action
been that the woman had had no time for alarm; moreover, she was not of the screaming kind: but now, as she
felt him endeavoring to disentangle his claws, and the
horrid sense of her fate smote her, and she saw instinctively the fierce plunge of those weapons, the long
strips of living flesh torn from her bones, the agony, the

quivering disgust, itself a worse agony,—while by her side, and holding her in his great lithe embrace, the monster crouched, his white tusks whetting and gnashing, his eyes glaring through all the darkness like balls of red fire,—a shriek, that rang in every forest hollow, that startled every winter-housed thing, that stirred and woke the least needle of the tasselled pines, tore through her lips. A moment afterward, the beast left the arm, once white, now crimson, and looked up alertly.

She did not think at this instant to call upon God. She called upon her husband. It seemed to her that she had but one friend in the world; that was he; and again the cry, loud, clear, prolonged, echoed through the woods. It was not the shriek that disturbed the creature at his relish; he was not born in the woods to be scared of an owl, you know; what then? It must have been the echo, most musical, most resonant, repeated and yet repeated, dying with long sighs of sweet sound, vibrated from rock to river and back again from depth to depth of cave and cliff. Her thought flew after it; she knew, that, even if her husband heard it, he yet could not reach her in time; she saw that while beast listened he would not gnaw,—and this she *felt* directly, when the rough, sharp, and multiplied stings of his tongue retouched her arm. Again her lips opened by instinct, but the sound that issued thence came by reason. She had heard that music charmed wild beasts,—just this point between life and death intensified every faculty,—and when she opened her lips the third time, it was not for shrieking, but for singing.

A little thread of melody stole out, a rill of tremulous motion; it was the cradle-song with which she rocked her baby;—how could she sing that? And then she remembered the baby sleeping rosily on the long settee before the fire,—the father cleaning his gun, with one foot on the green wooden rundle,—the merry light from the chimney dancing out and through the room, on the rafters of the ceiling with their tassels of onions and herbs, on the log walls painted with lichens and festooned with apples, on the king's-arm slung across the shelf with the old pirate's-cutlass, on the snow-pile of the bed, and on the great brass clock,—dancing, too, and lingering on the baby, with his fringed-gentian eyes, his chubby fists clenched on the pillow, and his fine breezy hair fanning with the motion of his father's foot. All this struck her in one, and made a sob of her breath, and she ceased.

Immediately the long red tongue thrust forth again. Before it touched, a song sprang to her lips, a wild sea-song, such as some sailor might be singing far out on trackless blue water that night, the shrouds whistling with frost and the sheets glued in ice,—a song with the wind in its burden and the spray in its chorus. The monster raised his head and flared the fiery eyeballs upon her, then fretted the imprisoned claws a moment and was quiet; only the breath like the vapor from some hell-pit still swathed her. Her voice, at first faint and fearful, gradually lost its quaver, grew under her control and subject to her modulation; it rose on long swells, it fell in subtile cadences, now and then its tones pealed out like bells from distant belfries on fresh sonorous mornings. She sung the song through, and, wondering lest his name of Indian Devil were not his true name, and if he would not detect her, she repeated it. Once or twice now, indeed, the beast stirred uneasily, turned, and made the bough sway at his movement. As she ended, he snapped his jaws together, and tore away the fettered member, curling it under him with a snarl,— when she burst into the gayest reel that ever answered a fiddle-bow. How many a time she had heard her husband play it on the homely fiddle made by himself from birch and cherrywood! how many a time she had seen

155

it danced on the floor of their one room, to the patter of
wooden clogs and the rustle of homespun petticoat!
how many a time she had danced it herself!—and did
she not remember once, as they joined clasps for eight-
hands-round, how it had lent its gay, bright measure to
her life? And here she was singing it alone, in the forest, at midnight, to a wild beast! As she sent her voice
trilling up and down its quick oscillations between joy
and pain, the creature who grasped her uncurled his
paw and scratched the bark from the bough; she must
vary the spell; and her voice spun leaping along the projecting points of tune of a hornpipe. Still singing, she
felt herself twisted about with a low growl and a lifting
of the red lip from the glittering teeth; she broke the
hornpipe's thread, and commenced unravelling a lighter,
livelier thing, an Irish jig. Up and down and round
about her voice flew, the beast threw back his head so
that the diabolical face fronted hers, and the torrent of
his breath prepared her for his feast as the anaconda
slimes his prey. Frantically she darted from tune to tune;
his restless movements followed her. She tired herself
with dancing and vivid national airs, growing feverish
and singing spasmodically as she felt her horrid tomb
yawning wider. Touching in this manner all the slogan
and keen clan cries, the beast moved again, but only to
lay the disengaged paw across her with heavy satisfaction. She did not dare to pause; through the clear cold
air, the frosty starlight, she sang. If there were yet any
tremor in the tone, it was not fear,—she had learned the
secret of sound at last; nor could it be chill,—far too
high a fever throbbed her pulses; it was nothing but the
thought of the log-house and of what might be passing
within it. She fancied the baby stirring in his sleep and
moving his pretty lips,—her husband rising and opening
the door, looking out after her, and wondering at her absence. She fancied the light pouring through the chink

and then shut in again with all the safety and comfort and joy, her husband taking down the fiddle and playing lightly with his head inclined, playing while she sang, while she sang for her life to an Indian Devil. Then she knew he was fumbling for and finding some shining fragment and scoring it down the yellowing hair, and unconsciously her voice forsook the wild wartunes and drifted into the half-gay, half-melancholy Rosin the Bow.

Suddenly she woke pierced with a pang, and the daggered tooth penetrating her flesh;—dreaming of safety, she had ceased singing and lost it. The beast has regained the use of all his limbs, and now, standing and raising his back, bristling and foaming, with sounds that would have been like hisses but for their deep and fearful sonority, he withdrew step by step toward the trunk of the tree, still with his flaming balls upon her. She was all at once free, on one end of the bough, twenty feet from the ground. She did not measure the distance, but rose to drop herself down, careless of any death, so that it were not this. Instantly, as if he scanned her thoughts, the creature bounded forward with a yell and caught her again in his dreadful hold. It might be that he was not greatly famished; for, as she suddenly flung up her voice again, he settled himself composedly on the bough, still clasping her with invincible pressure to his rough, ravenous breast, and listening in a fascination to the sad, strange U-la-lu that now moaned forth in loud, hollow tones above him. He half closed his eyes, and sleepily reopened and shut them again.

What rending pains were close at hand! Death! and what a death! worse than any other that is to be named! Water, be it cold or warm, that which buoys up blue icefields, or which bathes tropical coasts with currents of balmy bliss, is yet a gentle conqueror, kisses as it kills, and draws you down gently through darkening

157

fathoms to its heart. Death at the sword is the festival of
trumpet and bugle and banner, with glory ringing out
around you and distant hearts thrilling through yours.
No gnawing disease can bring such hideous end as this;
for that is a fiend bred of your own flesh, and this—is
it a fiend, this living lump of appetites? What dread
comes with the thought of perishing in flames! but fire,
let it leap and hiss never so hotly, is something too remote, too alien, to inspire us with such loathly horror as
a wild beast; if it have a life, that life is too utterly beyond our comprehension. Fire is not half ourselves; as
it devours, arouses neither hatred nor disgust; is not to
be known by the strength of our lower natures let loose;
does not drip our blood into our faces from foaming
chaps, nor mouth nor slaver above us with vitality. Let
us be ended by fire, and we are ashes, for the winds to
bear, the leaves to cover; let us be ended by wild beasts,
and the base, cursed thing howls with us forever
through the forest. All this she felt as she charmed him,
and what force it lent to her song God knows. If her
voice should fail! If the damp and cold should give her
any fatal hoarseness! If all the silent powers of the forest did not conspire to help her! The dark, hollow night
rose indifferently over her; the wide, cold air breathed
rudely past her, lifted her wet hair and blew it down
again; the great boughs swung with a ponderous
strength, now and then clashed their iron lengths together and shook off a sparkle of icy spears or some
long-lain weight of snow from their heavy shadows.
The green depths were utterly cold and silent and stern.
These beautiful haunts that all the summer were hers
and rejoiced to share with her their bounty, these heav-
ens that had yielded their largess, these stems that had
thrust their blossoms into her hands, all these friends of
three moons ago forgot her now and knew her no
longer.

Feeling her desolation, wild, melancholy, forsaken songs rose thereon from that frightful aerie,—weeping, wailing tunes, that sob among the people from age to age, and overflow with otherwise unexpressed sadness,—all rude, mournful ballads,—old tearful strains, that Shakespeare heard the vagrants sing, and that rise and fall like the wind and tide,—sailor-songs, to be heard only in lone mid-watches beneath the moon and stars,—ghastly rhyming romances, such as that famous one of the Lady Margaret, when

> "She slipped on her gown of green
> A piece below the knee,—
> And 't was all a long cold winter's night
> A dead corse followed she."

Still the beast lay with closed eyes, yet never relaxing his grasp. Once a half-whine of enjoyment escaped him,—he fawned his fearful head upon her; once he scored her cheek with his tongue; savage caresses that hurt like wounds. How weary she was! and yet how terribly awake! How fuller and fuller of dismay grew the knowledge that she was only prolonging her anguish and playing with death! How appalling the thought that with her voice ceased her existence! Yet she could not sing forever; her throat was dry and hard; her very breath was a pain; her mouth was hotter than any desert-worn pilgrim's;—if she could but drop upon her burning tongue one atom of the ice that glittered about her!—but both of her arms were pinioned in the giant's vice. She remembered the winding-sheet, and for the first time in her life shivered with spiritual fear. Was it hers? She asked herself, as she sang, what sins she had committed, what life she had led, to find her punishment so soon and in these pangs,—and then she sought eagerly for some reason why her husband was not up and abroad to find her. He failed her,—her one sole hope in life; and without being aware of it, her voice forsook the songs of suffering and sorrow for old Covenanting hymns,—hymns with which her mother had lulled her, which the class-leader pitched in the chimney-corners,—grand and sweet Methodist hymns, brimming with melody and with all fantastic involutions of tune to suit that ecstatic worship,—hymns full of the beauty of holiness, steadfast, relying, sanctified by the salvation they had lent to those in worse extremity than hers,—for they had found themselves in the grasp of hell, while she was but in the jaws of death. Out of this strange music, peculiar to one character of faith, and than which there is none more beautiful in its degree nor owning a more potent sway of sound, her voice soared into the glorified chants of churches. What to her was death by cold or famine or wild beasts? "Though He slay me, yet will I trust in him," she sang. High and clear through the frore fair night, the level moonbeams splintering in the wood, the scarce glints of stars in the shadowy roof of branches, these sacred anthems rose,— rose as a hope from despair, as some snowy spray of flower-bells from blackest mould. Was she not in God's hands? Did not the world swing at his will? If this were in his great plan of providence, was it not best, and should she not accept it?

"He is the Lord our God; his judgments are in all the earth."

Oh, sublime faith of our fathers, where utter self-sacrifice alone was true love, the fragrance of whose unrequired subjection was pleasanter than that of golden censers swung in purple-vapored chancels!

Never ceasing in the rhythm of her thoughts, articulated in music as they thronged, the memory of her first communion flashed over her. Again she was in that distant place on that sweet spring morning. Again the congregation rustled out, and the few remained, and she trembled to find herself among them. How well she remembered the devout, quiet faces, too accustomed to the sacred feast to glow with their inner joy! how well the snowy linen at the altar, the silver vessels slowly and silently shifting! and as the cup approached and passed, how the sense of delicious perfume stole in and heightened the transport of her prayer, and she had seemed, looking up through the windows where the sky soared blue in constant freshness, to feel all heaven's balms dripping from the portals, and to scent the lilies of eternal peace! Perhaps another would not have felt so much ecstasy as satisfaction on that occasion; but it is a true, if a later disciple, who has said, "The Lord bestoweth his blessings there, where he findeth the vessels empty."

"And does it need the walls of a church to renew my communion?" she asked. "Does not every moment stand a temple four-square to God? And in that morning, with its buoyant sunlight, was I any dearer to the Heart of the World than now?—'My beloved is mine, and I am his,' " she sang over and over again, with all varied inflection and profuse tune. How gently all the winter-wrapt things bent toward her then! into what relation with her had they grown! how this common dependence was the spell of their intimacy! how at one with Nature had she become! how all the night and the silence and the forest seemed to hold its breath, and to send its soul up to God in her singing! It was no longer despondency, that singing. It was neither prayer nor petition. She had left imploring, "How long wilt thou forget me, O Lord? Lighten mine eyes, lest I sleep the sleep of death! For in death there is no remembrance of thee,"—with countless other such fragments of supplication. She cried rather, "Yea, though I walk through the valley of the shadow of death, I will fear no evil: for thou art with me; thy rod and thy staff, they comfort me,"—and lingered, and repeated, and sang again, "I shall be satisfied, when I awake, with thy likeness."

Then she thought of the Great Deliverance, when he drew her up out of many waters, and the flashing old psalm pealed forth triumphantly:—

> "The Lord descended from above,
>   and bow'd the heavens hie:
> And underneath his feet he cast
>   the darknesse of the skie.
> On cherubs and on cherubins
>   full royally he road:
> And on the wings of all the winds
>   came flying all abroad."

She forgot how recently, and with what a strange pity for her own shapeless form that was to be, she had quaintly sung,—

> "O lovely appearance of death!
>   What sight upon earth is so fair?
> Not all the gay pageants that breathe
>   Can with a dead body compare!"

She remembered instead,—"In thy presence is fulness of joy; at thy right hand there are pleasures forevermore. God will redeem my soul from the power of the grave: for he shall receive me. He will swallow up death in victory." Not once now did she say, "Lord, how long wilt thou look on; rescue my soul from their destructions, my darling from the lions,"—for she knew that the young lions roar after their prey and seek their meat from God. "O Lord, thou preservest man and beast!" she said.

She had no comfort or consolation in this season,

such as sustained the Christian martyrs in the amphitheatre. She was not dying for her faith; there were no palms in heaven for her to wave; but how many a time had she declared,—"I had rather be a doorkeeper in the house of my God, than to dwell in the tents of wickedness!" And as the broad rays here and there broke through the dense covert of shade and lay in rivers of lustre on crystal sheathing and frozen fretting of trunk and limb and on the great spaces of refraction, they builded up visibly that house, the shining city on the hill, and singing, "Beautiful for situation, the joy of the whole earth, is Mount Zion, on the sides of the North, the city of the Great King," her vision climbed to that higher picture where the angle shows the dazzling thing, the holy Jerusalem descending out of heaven from God, with its splendid battlements and gates of pearls, and its foundations, the eleventh a jacinth, the twelfth an amethyst,—with its great white throne, and the rainbow round about it, in sight like unto an emerald: "And there shall be no night there,—for the Lord God giveth them light," she sang.

What whisper of dawn now rustled through the wilderness? How the night was passing! And still the beast crouched upon the bough, changing only the posture of his head, that again he might command her with those charmed eyes;—half their fire was gone, she could almost have released herself from his custody; yet, had she stirred, no one knows what malevolent instinct might have dominated anew. But of that she did not dream; long ago stripped of any expectation, she was experiencing in her divine rapture how mystically true it is that "he that dwelleth in the secret place of the Most High shall abide under the shadow of the Almighty."

Slow clarion cries now wound from the distance as the cocks caught the intelligence of day and re-echoed it faintly from farm to farm,—sleepy sentinels of night, sounding the foe's invasion, and translating that dim intuition to ringing notes of warning. Still she chatted on. A remote crash of brushwood told of some other beast on his depredations, or some night-belated traveller groping his way through the narrow path. Still she chanted on. The far, faint echoes of the chanticleers died into distance, the crashing of the branches grew nearer. No wild beast that, but a man's step,—a man's form in the moonlight, stalwart and strong,—on one arm slept a little child, in the other hand he held his gun. Still she chanted on.

Perhaps, when her husband last looked forth, he was half ashamed to find what a fear he felt for her. He knew she would never leave the child so long but for some direst need,—and yet he may have laughed at himself, as he lifted and wrapped it with awkward care, and, loading his gun and strapping on his horn, opened the door again and closed it behind him, going out and plunging into the darkness and dangers of the forest. He was more singularly alarmed than he would have been willing to acknowledge; as he had sat with his bow hovering over the strings, he had half believed to hear her voice mingling gayly with the instrument, till he paused and listened if she were not about to lift the latch and enter. As he drew nearer the heart of the forest, that intimation of melody seemed to grow more actual, to take body and breath, to come and go on long swells and ebbs of the night-breeze, to increase with tune and words, till a strange shrill singing grew ever clearer, and, as he stepped into an open space of moonbeams, far up in the branches, rocked by the wind, and singing, "How beautiful upon the mountains are the feet of him that bringeth good tidings, that publisheth peace," he saw his wife,—his wife,—but, great God in heaven! how? Some mad exclamation escaped him, but without diverting her. The child knew the singing voice, though never heard before in that unearthly key, and turned toward it through the veiling dreams. With a celerity almost instantaneous, it lay, in the twinkling of an eye, on the ground at the father's feet, while his gun was raised to his shoulder and levelled at the monster covering his wife with shaggy form and flaming gaze,—his wife so ghastly white, so rigid, so stained with blood, her eyes so fixedly bent above, and her lips, that had indurated into the chiselled pallor of marble, parted only with that flood of solemn song.

I do not know if it were the mother-instinct that for a moment lowered her eyes,—those eyes, so lately riveted on heaven, now suddenly seeing all life-long bliss possible. A thrill of joy pierced and shivered through her like a weapon, her voice trembled in its course, her glance lost its steady strength, fever-flushes chased each other over her face, yet she never once ceased chanting. She was quite aware, that, if her husband shot now, the ball must pierce her body before reaching any vital part of the beast,—and yet better that death, by his hand, than the other. But this her husband also knew, and he remained motionless, just covering the creature with the sight. He dared not fire, lest some wound not mortal should break the spell exercised by her voice, and the beast, enraged with pain, should rend her in atoms; moreover, the light was too uncertain for his aim. So he waited. Now and then he examined his gun to see if the damp were injuring its charge, now and then he wiped the great drops from his forehead. Again the cocks crowed with the passing hour,—the last time they were heard on that night. Cheerful home sound then, how full of safety and all comfort and rest it seemed! what sweet morning incidents of sparkling fire and sunshine, of gay

165

household bustle, shining dresser, and cooing baby, of steaming cattle in the yard, and brimming milk-pails at the door! what pleasant voices! what laughter! what security! and here—

Now, as she sang on in the slow, endless, infinite moments, the fervent vision of God's peace was gone. Just as the grave had lost its sting, she was snatched back again into the arms of earthly hope. In vain she tried to sing, "There remaineth a rest for the people of God,"—her eyes trembled on her husband's, and she could only think of him, and of the child, and of happiness that yet might be, but with what a dreadful gulf of doubt between! She shuddered now in the suspense; all calm forsook her; she was tortured with dissolving heats or frozen with icy blasts; her face contracted, growing small and pinched; her voice was hoarse and sharp,—every tone cut like a knife,—the notes became heavy to lift,—withheld by some hostile pressure,—impossible. One gasp, a convulsive effort, and there was silence,—she had lost her voice.

The beast made a sluggish movement,—stretched and fawned like one awaking,—then, as if he would have yet more of the enchantment, stirred her slightly with his muzzle. As he did so, a sidelong hint of the man standing below with the raised gun smote him; he sprung round furiously, and, seizing his prey, was about to leap into some unknown airy den of the topmost branches now waving to the slow dawn. The late moon had rounded through the sky so that her gleam at last fell full upon the bough with fairy frosting; the wintry morning light did not yet penetrate the gloom. The woman, suspended in mid-air an instant, cast only one agonized glance beneath,—but across and through it, ere the lids could fall, shot a withering sheet of flame,—a rifle-crack, half-heard, was lost in the terrible yell of desperation that bounded after it and filled her ears with savage echoes, and in the wide arc of some eternal descent she was falling;—but the beast fell under her.

I think that the moment following must have been too sacred for us, and perhaps the three have no special interest again till they issue from the shadows of the wilderness upon the white hills that skirt their home. The father carries the child hushed again into slumber, the mother follows with no such feeble step as might be anticipated. It is not time for reaction,—the tension not yet relaxed, the nerves still vibrant, she seems to herself like some one newly made; the night was a dream; the present stamped upon her in deep satisfaction, neither weighed nor compared with the past; if she has the careful tricks of former habit, it is as an automaton; and as they slowly climb the steep under the clear gray vault and the paling morning star, and as she stops to gather a spray of the red-rose berries or a feathery tuft of dead grasses for the chimney-piece of the log-house, or a handful of brown cones for the child's play,—of these quiet, happy folk you would scarcely dream how lately they had stolen from under the banner and encampment of the great King Death. The husband proceeds a step or two in advance; the wife lingers over a singular footprint in the snow, stoops and examines it, then looks up with a hurried word. Her husband stands alone on the hill, his arms folded across the babe, his gun fallen,—stands defined as a silhouette against the pallid sky. What is there in their home, lying below and yellowing in the light, to fix him with such a stare? She springs to his side. There is no home there. The log-house, the barns, the neighboring farms, the fences, are all blotted out and mingled in one smoking ruin. Desolation and death were indeed there, and beneficence and life in the forest. Tomahawk and scalping-knife, descending during that night, had left behind them only this work of their accomplished hatred and one subtle foot-print in the snow.

For the rest,—the world was all before them, where too choose.

KEN'S MYSTERY

Julian Hawthorne

O ne cool October evening—it was the last day of
the month, and unusually cool for the time of
year—I made up my mind to go and spend an
hour or two with my friend Keningale. Keningale was
an artist (as well as a musical amateur and poet), and
had a very delightful studio built onto his house, in
which he was wont to sit of an evening. The studio had
a cavernous fire-place, designed in imitation of the old-
fashioned fire-places of Elizabethan manor-houses, and
in it, when the temperature out-doors warranted, he
would build up a cheerful fire of dry logs. It would suit
me particularly well, I thought, to go and have a quiet
pipe and chat in front of that fire with my friend.

I had not had such a chat for a very long time—not,
in fact, since Keningale (or Ken, as his friends called
him) had returned from his visit to Europe the year before. He went abroad, as he affirmed at the time, "for
purposes of study," whereat we all smiled, for Ken, so

far as we knew him, was more likely to do anything else than to study. He was a young fellow of buoyant temperament, lively and social in his habits, of a brilliant and versatile mind, and possessing an income of twelve or fifteen thousand dollars a year; he could sing, play, scribble, and paint very cleverly, and some of his heads and figure-pieces were really well done, considering that he never had any regular training in art; but he was not a worker. Personally he was fine-looking, of good height and figure, active, healthy, and with a remarkably fine brow, and clear, full-gazing eye. Nobody was surprised at his going to Europe, nobody expected him to do anything there except amuse himself, and few anticipated that he would be soon again seen in New York. He was one of the sort that find Europe agree with them. Off he went, therefore; and in the course of a few months the rumor reached us that he was engaged to a handsome and wealthy New York girl whom he had met in London. This was nearly all we did hear of him until, not very long afterward, he turned up again on Fifth Avenue, to every one's astonishment; made no satisfactory answer to those who wanted to know how he happened to tire so soon of the Old World; while, as to the reported engagement, he cut short all allusion to that in so peremptory a manner as to show that it was not a permissible topic of conversation with him. It was surmised that the lady had jilted him; but, on the other hand, she herself returned home not a great while after, and, though she had plenty of opportunities, she has never married to this day.

Be the rights of that matter what they may, it was soon remarked that Ken was no longer the careless and merry fellow he used to be; on the contrary, he appeared grave, moody, averse from general society, and habitually taciturn and undemonstrative even in the company of his most intimate friends. Evidently something had happened to him, or he had done something. What? Had he committed a murder? or joined the Nihilists? or was his unsuccessful love affair at the bottom of it? Some declared that the cloud was only temporary, and would soon pass away. Nevertheless, up to the period of which I am writing, it had not passed away, but had rather gathered additional gloom, and threatened to become permanent.

Meanwhile I had met him twice or thrice at the club, at the opera, or in the street, but had as yet had no opportunity of regularly renewing my acquaintance with him. We had been on a footing of more than common intimacy in the old days, and I was not disposed to think that he would refuse to renew the former relations now. But what I had heard and myself seen of his changed condition imparted a stimulating tinge of suspense or curiosity to the pleasure with which I looked forward to the prospects of this evening. His house stood at a distance of two or three miles beyond the general range of habitations in New York at this time, and as I walked briskly along in the clear twilight air I had leisure to go over in my mind all that I had known of Ken and had divined of his character. After all, had there not always been something in his nature—deep down, and held in abeyance by the activity of his animal spirits—but something strange and separate, and capable of developing under suitable conditions into—into what? As I asked myself this question I arrived at his door; and it was with a feeling of relief that I felt the next moment the cordial grasp of his hand, and his voice bidding me welcome in a tone that indicated unaffected gratification at my presence. He drew me at once into the studio, relieved me of my hat and cane, and then put his hand on my shoulder.

"I am glad to see you," he repeated, with singular

earnestness—"glad to see you and to feel you; and to-night of all nights in the year."

"Why to-night especially?"

"Oh, never mind. It's just as well, too, you didn't let me know beforehand you were coming; the unreadiness is all, to paraphrase the poet. Now, with you to help me, I can drink a glass of whisky and water and take a bit draw of the pipe. This would have been a grim night for me if I'd been left to myself."

"In such a lap of luxury as this, too!" said I, looking round at the glowing fire-place, the low, luxurious chairs, and all the rich and sumptuous fittings of the room. "I should have thought a condemned murderer might make himself comfortable here."

"Perhaps; but that's not exactly my category at present. But have you forgotten what night this is? This is November-eve, when, as tradition asserts, the dead arise and walk about, and fairies, goblins, and spiritual beings of all kinds have more freedom and power than on any other day of the year. One can see you've never been in Ireland."

"I wasn't aware till now that you had been there, either."

"Yes, I have been in Ireland. Yes—" He paused, sighed, and fell into a reverie, from which, however, he soon roused himself by an effort, and went to a cabinet in a corner of the room for the liquor and tobacco. While he was thus employed I sauntered about the studio, taking note of the various beauties, grotesquenesses, and curiosities that it contained. Many things were there to repay study and arouse admiration; for Ken was a good collector, having excellent taste as well as means to back it. But, upon the whole, nothing interested me more than some studies of a female head, roughly done in oils, and, judging from the sequestered positions in which I found them, not intended by the artist for exhibition or criticism. There were three or four of these studies, all of the same face, but in different poses and costumes. In one the head was enveloped in a dark hood, overshadowing and partly concealing the features; in another she seemed to be peering duskily through a latticed casement, lit by a faint moonlight; a third showed her splendidly attired in evening costume, with jewels in her hair and ears, and sparkling on her snowy bosom. The expressions were as various as the poses; now it was demure penetration, now a subtle inviting glance, now burning passion, and again a look of elfish and elusive mockery. In whatever phase, the countenance possessed a singular and poignant fascination, not of beauty merely, though that was very striking, but of character and quality likewise.

"Did you find this model abroad?" I inquired at length. "She has evidently inspired you, and I don't wonder at it."

Ken, who had been mixing the punch, and had not noticed my movements, now looked up, and said: "I didn't mean those to be seen. They don't satisfy me, and I am going to destroy them; but I couldn't rest till I'd made some attempts to reproduce— What was it you asked? Abroad? yes—or no. They were all painted here within the last six weeks."

"Whether they satisfy you or not, they are by far the best things of yours I have ever seen."

"Well, let them alone, and tell me what you think of this beverage. To my thinking, it goes to the right spot. It owes its existence to your coming here. I can't drink alone, and those portraits are not company, though, for aught I know, she might have come out of the canvas to-night and sat down in that chair." Then, seeing my inquiring look, he added, with a hasty laugh, "It's November-eve, you know, when anything may happen, provided its strange enough. Well, here's to ourselves."

We each swallowed a deep draught of the smoking and aromatic liquor, and set down our glasses with approval. The punch was excellent. Ken now opened a box of cigars, and we seated ourselves before the fireplace.

"All we need now," I remarked, after a short silence, "is a little music. By-the-by, Ken, have you still got the banjo I gave you before you went abroad?"

He paused so long before replying that I supposed he had not heard my question. "I have got it," he said, at length, "but it will never make any more music."

"Got broken, eh? Can't it be mended? It was a fine instrument."

"It's not broken, but it's past mending. You shall see for yourself."

He arose as he spoke, and going to another part of the studio, opened a black oak coffer, and took out of it a long object wrapped up in a piece of faded yellow silk. He handed it to me, and when I had unwrapped it, there appeared a thing that might once have been a banjo, but had little resemblance to one now. It bore every sign of extreme age. The wood of the handle was honey-combed with the gnawings of worms, and dusty with dry-rot. The parchment head was green with mold, and hung in shriveled tatters. The hoop, which was of solid silver, was so blackened and tarnished that it looked like dilapidated iron. The strings were gone, and most of the tuning-screws had dropped out of their decayed sockets. Altogether it had the appearance of having been made before the Flood, and been forgotten in the forecastle of Noah's Ark ever since.

"It is a curious relic, certainly," I said. "Where did you come across it? I had no idea that the banjo was invented so long ago as this. It certainly can't be less than two hundred years old, and may be much older than that."

Ken smiled gloomily. "You are quite right," he said; "it is at least two hundred years old, and yet it is the very same banjo that you gave me a year ago."

"Hardly," I returned, smiling in my turn, "since that was made to my order with a view to presenting it to you."

"I know that; but the two hundred years have passed since then. Yes; it is absurd and impossible, I know, but nothing is truer. That banjo, which was made last year, existed in the sixteenth century, and has been rotting ever since. Stay. Give it to me a moment, and I'll convince you. You recollect that your name and mine, with the date, were engraved on the silver hoop?"

"Yes; and there was a private mark of my own there, also."

"Very well," said Ken, who had been rubbing a place on the hoop with a corner of the yellow silk wrapper; "look at that."

I took the decrepit instrument from him, and examined the spot which he had rubbed. It was incredible, sure enough; but there wee the names and the date precisely as I had caused them to be engraved; and there, moreover, was my own private mark, which I had idly made with an old etching point not more than eighteen months before. After convincing myself that there was no mistake, I laid the banjo across my knees, and stared at my friend in bewilderment. He sat smoking with a kind of grim composure, his eyes fixed upon the blazing logs.

"I'm mystified, I confess," said I. "Come; what is the joke? What method have you discovered of producing the decay of centuries on this unfortunate banjo in a few months? And why did you do it? I have heard of an elixir to counteract the effects of time, but your recipe seems to work the other way—to make time rush forward at two hundred times his usual rate, in one place,

175

while he jogs on at his usual gait elsewhere. Unfold your mystery, magician. Seriously, Ken, how on earth did the thing happen?"

"I know no more about it than you do," was his reply. "Either you and I and all the rest of the living world are insane, or else there has been wrought a miracle as strange as any in tradition. How can I explain it? It is a common saying—a common experience, if you will—that we may, on certain trying or tremendous occasions, live years in one moment. But that's a mental experience, not a physical one, and one that applies, at all events, only to human beings, not to senseless things of wood and metal. You imagine the thing is some trick or jugglery. If it be, I don't know the secret of it. There's no chemical appliance that I ever heard of that will get a piece of solid wood into that condition in a few months, or a few years. And it wasn't done in a few years, or a few months either. A year ago to-day at this very hour that banjo was as sound as when it left the maker's hands, and twenty-four hours afterward—I'm telling you the simple truth—it was as you see it now."

The gravity and earnestness with which Ken made this astounding statement were evidently not assumed. He believed every word that he uttered. I knew not what to think. Of course my friend might be insane, though he betrayed none of the ordinary symptoms of mania; but, however that might be, there was the banjo, a witness whose silent testimony there was no gainsaying. The more I meditated on the matter the more inconceivable did it appear. Two hundred years— twenty-four hours; these were the terms of the proposed equation. Ken and the banjo both affirmed that the equation had been made; all worldly knowledge and experience affirmed it to be impossible. What was the explanation? What is time? What is life? I felt myself beginning to doubt the reality of all things. And so this was the mystery which my friend had been brooding over since his return from abroad. No wonder it had changed him. More to be wondered at was it that it had not changed him more.

"Can you tell me the whole story?" I demanded at length.

Ken quaffed another draught from his glass of whisky and water and rubbed his hand through his thick brown beard. "I have never spoken to any one of it heretofore," he said, "and I had never meant to speak of it. But I'll try and give you some idea of what it was. You know me better than any one else; you'll understand the thing as far as it can ever be understood, and perhaps I may be relieved of some of the oppression it has caused me. For it is rather a ghastly memory to grapple with alone, I can tell you."

Hereupon, without further preface, Ken related the following tale. He was, I may observe in passing, a naturally fine narrator. There were deep, lingering tones in his voice, and he could strikingly enhance the comic or pathetic effect of a sentence by dwelling here and there upon some syllable. His features were equally susceptible of humorous and of solemn expressions, and his eyes were in form and hue wonderfully adapted to showing great varieties of emotion. Their mournful aspect was extremely earnest and affecting; and when Ken was giving utterance to some mysterious passage of the tale they had a doubtful, melancholy, exploring look which appealed irresistibly to the imagination. But the interest of his story was too pressing to allow of noticing these incidental embellishments at the time, though they doubtless had their influence upon me all the same.

"I left New York on an Inman Line steamer, you remember," began Ken, "and landed at Havre. I went the usual round of sight-seeing on the Continent, and got round to London in July, at the height of the season. I had good introductions, and met any number of agreeable and famous people. Among others was a young lady, a countrywoman of my own—you know whom I mean—who interested me very much, and before her family left London she and I were engaged. We parted there for the time, because she had the Continental trip still to make, while I wanted to take the opportunity to visit the north of England and Ireland. I landed at Dublin about the 1st of October, and, zigzagging about the country, I found myself in County Cork about two weeks later.

"There is in that region some of the most lovely scenery that human eyes ever rested on, and it seems to be less known to tourists than many places of infinitely less picturesque value. A lonely region too: during my rambles I met not a single stranger like myself, and few enough natives. It seems incredible that so beautiful a country should be so deserted. After walking a dozen Irish miles you come across a group of two or three one-roomed cottages, and, like as not, one or more of those will have the roof off and the walls in ruins. The few peasants whom one sees, however, are affable and hospitable, especially when they hear you are from that terrestrial heaven whither most of their friends and relatives have gone before them. They seem simple and primitive enough at first sight, and yet they are as strange and incomprehensible a race as any in the world. They are as superstitious, as credulous of marvels, fairies, magicians, and omens, as the men whom St. Patrick preached to, and at the same time they are shrewd, skeptical, sensible, and bottomless liars. Upon the whole, I met with no nation on my travels whose company I enjoyed so much, or who inspired me with so much kindliness, curiosity, and repugnance.

"At length I got to a place on the sea-coast, which I

will not further specify than to say that it is not many miles from Ballymacheen, on the south shore. I have seen Venice and Naples, I have driven along the Cornice Road, I have spent a month at our own Mount Desert, and I say that all of them together are not so beautiful as this glowing, deep-hued, soft-gleaming, silvery-lighted, ancient harbor and town, with the tall hills crowding round it and the black cliffs and headlands planting their iron feet in the blue, transparent sea. It is a very old place, and has had a history which it has outlived ages since. It may once have had two or three thousand inhabitants; it has scarce five or six hundred to-day. Half the houses are in ruins or have disappeared; many of the remainder are standing empty. All the people are poor, most of them abjectly so; they saunter about with bare feet and uncovered heads, the women in quaint black or dark-blue cloaks, the men in such anomalous attire as only an Irishman knows how to get together, the children half naked. The only comfortable-looking people are the monks and the priests, and the soldiers in the fort. For there is a fort there, constructed on the huge ruins of one which may have done duty in the reign of Edward the Black Prince, or earlier, in whose mossy embrasures are mounted a couple of cannon, which occasionally sent a practice-shot or two at the cliff on the other side of the harbor. The garrison consists of a dozen men and three or four officers and non-commissioned officers. I suppose they are relieved occasionally, but those I saw seemed to have become component parts of their surroundings.

"I put up at a wonderful little old inn, the only one in the place, and took my meals in a dining-saloon fifteen feet by nine, with a portrait of George I (a print varnished to preserve it) hanging over the mantel-piece. On the second evening after dinner a young gentleman came in—the dining-saloon being public property of course—and ordered some bread and cheese and a bottle of Dublin stout. We presently fell into talk; he turned out to be an officer from the fort, Lieutenant O'Connor, and a fine young specimen of the Irish soldier he was. After telling me all he' knew about the town, the surrounding country, his friends, and himself, he intimated a readiness to sympathize with whatever tale I might choose to pour into his ear; and I had pleasure in trying to rival his own outspokenness. We became excellent friends; we had up a half-pint of Kinahan's whisky, and the lieutenant expressed himself in terms of high praise of my countrymen, my country, and my own particular cigars. When it became time for him to depart I accompanied him—for there was a splendid moon abroad— and bade him farewell at the fort entrance, having promised to come over the next day and make the acquaintance of the other fellows. 'And mind your eye, now, going back, my dear boy,' he called out, as I turned my face homeward. 'Faith, 'tis a spooky place, that graveyard, and you'll as likely meet the black woman there as anywhere else!'

"The graveyard was a forlorn and barren spot on the hill-side, just the hither side of the fort: thirty or forty rough head-stones, few of which retained any semblance of the perpendicular, while many were so shattered and decayed as to seem nothing more than irregular natural projections from the ground. Who the black woman might be I knew not, and did not stay to inquire. I had never been subject to ghostly apprehensions, and as a matter of fact, though the path I had to follow was in places very bad going, not to mention a hap-hazard scramble over a ruined bridge that covered a deep-lying brook, I reached my inn without any adventure whatever.

"The next day I kept my appointment at the fort, and found no reason to regret it; and my friendly sentiments were abundantly reciprocated, thanks more especially, perhaps, to the success of my banjo, which I carried with me, and which was as novel as it was popular with those who listened to it. The chief personages in the social circle besides my friend the lieutenant were Major Molloy, who was in command, a racy and juicy old campaigner, with a face like a sunset, and the surgeon, Dr. Dudeen, a long, dry, humorous genius, with a wealth of anecdotal and traditional lore at his command that I have never seen surpassed. We had a jolly time of it, and it was the precursor of many more like it. The remains of October slipped away rapidly, and I was obliged to remember that I was a traveler in Europe, and not a resident in Ireland. The major, the surgeon, and the lieutenant all protested cordially against my proposed departure, but, as there was no help for it, they arranged a farewell dinner to take place in the fort on All-halloween.

"I wish you could have been at that dinner with me! It was the essence of Irish good-fellowship. Dr. Dudeen was in great force; the major was better than the best of Lever's novels; the lieutenant was overflowing with hearty good-humor, merry chaff, and sentimental rhapsodies anent this or the other pretty girl of the neighborhood. For my part I made the banjo ring as it had never rung before, and the others joined in the chorus with a mellow strength of lungs such as you don't often hear outside of Ireland. Among the stories that Dr. Dudeen regaled us with was one about the Kern of Querin and his wife, Ethelind Fionguala—which being interpreted signified 'the white-shouldered.' The lady, it appears, was originally betrothed to one O'Connor (here the lieutenant smacked his lips), but was stolen away on the wedding night by a party of vampires, who, it would seem, where at that period a prominent feature among the troubles of Ireland. But as they were bearing her along—she being unconscious—to that supper where she was not to eat but to be eaten, the young Kern of Querin, who happened to be out duck-shooting, met the party, and emptied his gun at it. The vampires fled, and the Kern carried the fair lady, still in a state of insensibility, to his house. 'And by the same token, Mr. Keningale,' observed the doctor, knocking the ashes out of his pipe, 'ye're after passing that very house on your way here. The one with the dark archway underneath it, and the big mullioned window at the corner, ye recollect, hanging over the street as I might say—'

" 'Go 'long wid the house, Dr. Dudeen, dear,' interrupted the lieutenant; 'sure can't you see we're all dying to know what happened to sweet Miss Fionguala, God be good to her, when I was after getting her safe up-stairs—'

" 'Faith, then, I can tell ye that myself, Mr. O'Connor,' exclaimed the major, imparting a rotary motion to the remnants of whisky in his tumbler. ' 'Tis a question to be solved on general principles, as Colonel O'Halloran said that time he was asked what he'd do if he'd been the Dook o'Wellington, and the Prussians hadn't come up in the nick o' time at Waterloo. 'Faith,' says the colonel, 'I'll tell ye—'

" 'Arrah, then, major, why would ye be interruptin' the doctor, and Mr. Keningale there lettin' his glass stay empty till he hears—The Lord save us! the bottle's empty!'

"In the excitement consequent upon this discovery, the thread of the doctor's story was lost; and before it could be recovered the evening had advanced so far that I felt obliged to withdraw. It took some time to make my proposition heard and comprehended; and a still longer time to put it in execution; so that it was fully midnight before I found myself standing in the cool pure air outside the fort, with the farewells of my boon companions ringing in my ears.

"Considering that it had been rather a wet evening indoors, I was in a remarkably good state of preservation, and I therefore ascribed it rather to the roughness of the road than to the smoothness of the liquor, when, after advancing a few rods, I stumbled and fell. As I picked myself up I fancied I had heard a laugh, and supposed that the lieutenant, who had accompanied me to the gate, was making merry over my mishap; but on looking round I saw that the gate was closed and no one was visible. The laugh, moreover, had seemed to be close at hand, and to be even pitched in a key that was rather feminine than masculine. Of course I must have been deceived; nobody was near me: my imagination had played me a trick, or else there was more truth than poetry in the tradition that Halloween is the carnival-time of disembodied spirits. It did not occur to me at the time that a stumble is held by the superstitious Irish to be an evil omen, and had I remembered it it would only have been to laugh at it. At all events, I was physically none the worse for my fall, and I resumed my way immediately.

"But the path was singularly difficult to find, or rather the path I was following did not seem to be the right one. I did not recognize it; I could have sworn (except I knew the contrary) that I had never seen it before. The moon had risen, though her light was as yet obscured by clouds, but neither my immediate surroundings nor the general aspect of the region appeared familiar. Dark, silent hill-sides mounted up on either hand, and the road, for the most part, plunged downward, as if to conduct me into the bowels of the earth. The place was alive with strange echoes, so that at times I seemed to be walking through the midst of muttering voices and mysterious whispers, and a wild, faint sound of laughter seemed ever and anon to reverberate among the passes of the hills. Currents of colder air sighing up through narrow defiles and dark crevices touched my face as with airy fingers. A certain feeling of anxiety and insecurity began to take possession of me, though there was no definable cause for it, unless that I might be belated in getting home. With the perverse instinct of those who are lost I hastened my steps, but was impelled now and then to glance back over my shoulder, with a sensation of being pursued. But no living creature was in sight. The moon, however, had now risen higher, and the clouds that were drifting slowly across the sky flung into the naked valley dusky shadows, which occasionally assumed shapes that looked like the vague semblance of gigantic human forms.

"How long I had been hurrying onward I know not, when, with a kind of suddenness, I found myself approaching a graveyard. It was situated on the spur of a hill, and there was no fence around it, nor anything to protect it from the incursions of passers-by. There was something in the general appearance of this spot that made me half fancy I had seen it before; and I should have taken it to be the same that I had often noticed on my way to the fort, but that the latter was only a few hundred yards distant therefrom, whereas I must have traversed several miles at least. As I drew near, moreover, I observed that the head-stones did not appear so ancient and decayed as those of the other. But what chiefly attracted my attention was the figure that was leaning or half sitting upon one of the largest of the upright slabs near the road. It was a female figure draped in black, and a closer inspection—for I was soon within a few yards of her—showed that she wore the calla, or long hooded cloak, the most common as well as the most ancient garment of Irish women, and doubtless of Spanish origin.

"I was a trifle startled by this apparition, so unexpected as it was, and so strange did it seem that any human creature should be at that hour of the night in so desolate and sinister a place. Involuntarily I paused as I came opposite her, and gazed at her intently. But the moonlight fell behind her, and the deep hood of her cloak so completely shadowed her face that I was unable to discern anything but the sparkle of a pair of eyes, which appeared to be returning my gaze with much vivacity.

" 'You seem to be at home here,' I said, at length. 'Can you tell me where I am?'

"Hereupon the mysterious personage broke into a light laugh, which, though in itself musical and agreeable, was of a timbre and intonation that caused my heart to beat rather faster than my late pedestrian exertions warranted; for it was the identical laugh (or so my imagination persuaded me) that had echoed in my ears as I arose from my tumble an hour or two ago. For the rest, it was the laugh of a young woman, and presumably of a pretty one; and yet it had a wild, airy, mocking quality, that seemed hardly human at all, or not, at any rate, characteristic of a being of affections and limitations like unto ours. But this impression of mine was fostered, no doubt, by the unusual and uncanny circumstances of the occasion.

" 'Sure, sir,' said she, 'you're at the grave of Ethelind Fionguala.'

"As she spoke she rose to her feet, and pointed to the inscription on the stone. I bent forward, and was able, without much difficulty, to decipher the name, and a date which indicated that the occupant of the grave must have entered the disembodied state between two and three centuries ago.

" 'And who are you?' was my next question.

185

" 'I'm called Elsie,' she replied. 'But where would your honor be going November-eve?'

"I mentioned my destination, and asked her whether she could direct me thither.

" 'Indeed, then, 'tis there I'm going myself,' Elsie replied; 'and if your honor 'll follow me, and play me a tune on the pretty instrument, 'tisn't long we'll be on the road.'

"She pointed to the banjo which I carried wrapped up under my arm. How she knew that it was a musical instrument I could not imagine; possibly, I thought, she may have seen me playing on it as I strolled about the environs of the town. Be that as it may, I offered no opposition to the bargain, and further intimated that I would reward her more substantially on our arrival. At that she laughed again, and made a peculiar gesture with her hand above her head. I uncovered my banjo, swept my fingers across the strings, and struck into a fantastic dance-measure, to the music of which we proceeded along the path, Elsie slightly in advance, her feet keeping time to the airy measure. In fact, she trod so lightly, with an elastic, undulating movement, that with a little more it seemed as if she might float onward like a spirit. The extreme whiteness of her feet attracted my eye, and I was surprised to find that instead of being bare, as I had supposed, these were incased in white satin slippers quaintly embroidered with gold thread.

" 'Elsie,' said I, lengthening my steps so as to come up with her, 'where do you live, and what do you do for a living?'

" 'Sure, I live by myself,' she answered; 'and if you'd be after knowing how, you must come and see for yourself.'

" 'Are you in the habit of walking over the hills at night in shoes like that?'

" 'And why would I not?' she asked, in her turn.

'And where did your honor get the pretty gold ring on your finger?'

"The ring, which was of no great intrinsic value, had struck my eye in an old curiosity-shop in Cork. It was an antique of very old-fashioned design, and might have belonged (as the vender assured me was the case) to one of the early kings or queens of Ireland.

" 'Do you like it?' said I.

" 'Will your honor be after making a present of it to Elsie?' she returned, with an insinuating tone and turn of the head.

" 'Maybe I will, Elsie, on one condition. I am an artist; I make pictures of people. If you will promise to come to my studio and let me paint your portrait, I'll give you the ring, and some money besides.'

" 'And will you give me the ring now?' said Elsie.

" 'Yes, if you'll promise.'

" 'And will you play the music to me?' she continued.

" 'As much as you like.'

" 'But maybe I'll not be handsome enough for ye,' said she, with a glance of her eyes beneath the dark hood.

" 'I'll take the risk of that,' I answered, laughing, 'though, all the same, I don't mind taking a peep beforehand to remember you by.' So saying, I put forth a hand to draw back the concealing hood. But Elsie eluded me, I scarce know how, and laughed a third time, with the same airy, mocking cadence.

" 'Give me the ring first, and then you shall see me,' she said, coaxingly.

" 'Stretch out your hand, then,' returned I, removing the ring from my finger. 'When we are better acquainted, Elsie, you won't be so suspicious.'

"She held out a slender, delicate hand, on the forefinger of which I slipped the ring. As I did so, the folds of

187

her cloak fell a little apart, affording me a glimpse of a white shoulder and of a dress that seemed in that deceptive semi-darkness to be wrought of rich and costly material; and I caught, too, or so I fancied, the frosty sparkle of precious stones.

" 'Arrah, mind where ye tread!' said Elsie, in a sudden, sharp tone.

"I looked round, and became aware for the first time that we were standing near the middle of a ruined bridge which spanned a rapid stream that flowed at a considerable depth below. The parapet of the bridge on one side was broken down, and I must have been, in fact, in imminent danger of stepping over into empty air. I made my way cautiously across the decaying structure; but, when I turned to assist Elsie, she was nowhere to be seen.

"What had become of the girl? I called, but no answer came. I gazed about on every side, but no trace of her was visible. Unless she had plunged into the narrow abyss at my feet, there was no place where she could have concealed herself—none at least that I could discover. She had vanished, nevertheless; and since her disappearance must have been premeditated, I finally came to the conclusion that it was useless to attempt to find her. She would present herself again in her own good time, or not at all. She had given me the slip very cleverly, and I must make the best of it. The adventure was perhaps worth the ring.

"On resuming my way, I was not a little relieved to find that I once more knew where I was. The bridge that I had just crossed was none other than the one I mentioned some time back; I was within a mile of the town, and my way lay clear before me. The moon, moreover, had now quite dispersed the clouds, and shone down with exquisite brilliance. Whatever her other failings, Elsie had been a trustworthy guide; she had brought me out of the depth of elf-land into the material world again. It had been a singular adventure, certainly; and I mused over it with a sense of mysterious pleasure as I sauntered along, humming snatches of airs, and accompanying myself on the strings. Hark! what light step was that behind me? It sounded like Elsie's; but no, Elsie was not there. The same impression or hallucination, however, recurred several times before I reached the outskirts of the town—the tread of an airy foot behind or beside my own. The fancy did not make me nervous; on the contrary, I was pleased with the notion of being thus haunted, and gave myself up to a romantic and genial vein of reverie.

"After passing one or two roofless and moss-grown cottages, I entered the narrow and rambling street which leads through the town. This street a short distance down widens a little, as if to afford the wayfarer space to observe a remarkable old house that stands on the northern side. The house was built of stone, and in a noble style of architecture; it reminded me somewhat of certain palaces of the old Italian nobility that I had seen on the Continent, and it may very probably have been built by one of the Italian or Spanish immigrants of the sixteenth or seventeenth century. The molding of the projecting windows and arched doorway was richly carved, and upon the front of the building was an escutcheon wrought in high relief, though I could not make out the purport of the device. The moonlight falling upon this picturesque pile enhanced all its beauties, and at the same time made it seem like a vision that might dissolve away when the light ceased to shine. I must often have seen the house before, and yet I retained no definite recollection of it; I had never until now examined it with my eyes open, so to speak. Leaning against the wall on the opposite side of the street, I contemplated it for a long while at my leisure. The window at the corner was really a very fine and massive affair. It projected over the pavement below, throwing a heavy shadow aslant; the frames of the diamond-paned lattices were heavily mullioned. How often in past ages had that lattice been pushed open by some fair hand, revealing to a lover waiting beneath in the moonlight the charming countenance of his high-born mistress! Those were brave days. They had passed away long since. The great house had stood empty for who could tell how many years; only bats and vermin were its inhabitants. Where now were those who had built it? and who were they? Probably the very name of them was forgotten.

"As I continued to stare upward, however, a conjecture presented itself to my mind which rapidly ripened into a conviction. Was not this the house that Dr. Dudeen had described that very evening as having been formerly the abode of the Kern of Querin and his mysterious bride? There was the projecting window, the arched doorway. Yes, beyond a doubt this was the very house. I emitted a low exclamation of renewed interest and pleasure, and my speculations took a still more imaginative, but also a more definite turn.

"What had been the fate of that lovely lady after the Kern had brought her home insensible in his arms? Did she recover, and were they married and made happy ever after; or had the sequel been a tragic one? I remembered to have read that the victims of vampires generally became vampires themselves. Then my thoughts went back to that grave on the hill-side. Surely that was unconsecrated ground. Why had they buried her there? Ethelind of the white shoulder! Ah! why had not I lived in those days; or why might not some magic cause them to live again for me? Then would I seek this street at midnight, and standing here beneath her window, I would lightly touch the strings of my bandore until the casement opened cautiously and she looked down. A sweet vision indeed! And what prevented my realizing it? Only a matter of a couple of centuries or so. And was time, then, at which poets and philosophers sneer, so rigid and real a matter that a little faith and imagination might not overcome it? At all events, I had my banjo, the bandore's legitimate and lineal descendant, and the memory of Fionguala should have the love-ditty.

"Hereupon, having retuned the instrument, I launched forth into an old Spanish love-song, which I had met with in some moldy library during my travels, and had set to music of my own. I sang low, for the deserted street re-echoed the lightest sound, and what I sang must reach only my lady's ears. The words were warm with the fire of the ancient Spanish chivalry, and I threw into their expression all the passion of the lovers of romance. Surely Fionguala, the white-shouldered, would hear, and awaken from her sleep of centuries, and come to the latticed casement and look down! Hist! see yonder! What light—what shadow is that that seems to flit from room to room within the abandoned house, and now approaches the mullioned window? Are my eyes dazzled by the play of the moonlight, or does the casement move—does it open? Nay, this is no delusion; there is no error of the senses here. There is simply a woman, young, beautiful, and richly attired, bending forward from the window, and silently beckoning me to approach.

"Too much amazed to be conscious of amazement, I advanced until I stood directly beneath the casement, and the lady's face, as she stooped toward me, was not more than twice a man's height from my own. She smiled and kissed her finger-tips; something white fluttered in her hand, then fell through the air to the ground at my feet. The next moment she had withdrawn, and I heard the lattice close.

"I picked up what she had let fall; it was a delicate lace handkerchief, tied to the handle of an elaborately wrought bronze key. It was evidently the key of the house, and invited me to enter. I loosened it from the handkerchief, which bore a faint, delicious perfume, like the aroma of flowers in an ancient garden, and turned to the arched doorway. I felt no misgiving, and scarcely any sense of strangeness. All was as I had wished it to be, and as it should be; the medieval age was alive once more, and as for myself, I almost felt the velvet cloak hanging from my shoulder and the long rapier dangling at my belt. Standing in front of the door I thrust the key into the lock, turned it, and felt the bolt yield. The next instant the door was opened, apparently from within; I stepped across the threshold, the door closed again, and I was alone in the house, and in darkness.

"Not alone, however! As I extended my hand to grope my way it was met by another hand, soft, slender, and cold, which insinuated itself gently into mine and drew me forward. Forward I went, nothing loath; the darkness was impenetrable, but I could hear the light rustle of a dress close to me, and the same delicious perfume that had emanated from the handkerchief enriched the air that I breathed, while the little hand that clasped and was clasped by my own alternately tightened and half relaxed the hold of its soft cold fingers. In this manner, and treading lightly, we traversed what I presumed to be a long, irregular passageway, and ascended a staircase. Then another corridor, until finally we paused, a door opened, emitting a flood of soft light, into which we entered, still hand in hand. The darkness and the doubt were at an end.

"The room was of imposing dimensions, and was furnished and decorated in a style of antique splendor. The walls were draped with mellow hues of tapestry; clusters of candles burned in polished silver sconces, and were reflected and multiplied in tall mirrors placed in the four corners of the room. The heavy beams of the dark oaken ceiling crossed each other in squares, and were laboriously carved; the curtains and the drapery of the chairs were of heavy-figured damask. At one end of the room was a broad ottoman, and in front of it a table, on which was set forth, in massive silver dishes, a sumptuous repast, with wines in crystal beakers. At the side was a vast and deep fire-place, with space enough on the broad hearth to burn whole trunks of trees. No fire, however, was there, but only a great heap of dead embers; and the room, for all its magnificence, was cold—cold as a tomb, or as my lady's hand—and it sent a subtle chill creeping to my heart.

"But my lady! how fair she was! I gave but a passing glance at the room; my eyes and my thoughts were all for her. She was dressed in white, like a bride; diamonds sparkled in her dark hair and on her snowy bosom; her lovely face and slender lips were pale, and all the paler for the dusky glow of her eyes. She gazed at me with a strange, elusive smile; and yet there was, in her aspect and bearing, something familiar in the midst of strangeness, like the burden of a song heard long ago and recalled among other conditions and surroundings. It seemed to me that something in me recognized her and knew her, had known her always. She was the woman of whom I had dreamed, whom I had beheld in visions, whose voice and face had haunted me from boyhood up. Whether we had ever met before, as human beings meet, I knew not; perhaps I had been blindly seeking her all over the world, and she had been awaiting me in this splendid room, sitting by those dead embers until all the warmth had gone out of her blood, only to be restored by the heat with which my love might supply her.

" 'I thought you had forgotten me,' she said, nodding as if in answer to my thought. 'The night was so late—our one night of the year! How my heart rejoiced when I heard your dear voice singing the song I know so well! Kiss me—my lips are cold!'

"Cold indeed they were—cold as the lips of death. But the warmth of my own seemed to revive them. They were now tinged with a faint color, and in her cheeks also appeared a delicate shade of pink. She drew fuller breath, as one who recovers from a long lethargy. Was it my life that was feeding her? I was ready to give her all. She drew me to the table and pointed to the viands and the wine.

" 'Eat and drink,' she said. 'You have traveled far, and you need food.'

" 'Will you eat and drink with me?' said I, pouring out the wine.

" 'You are the only nourishment I want,' was her answer. 'This wine is thin and cold. Give me wine as red as your blood and as warm, and I will drain a goblet to the dregs.'

"At these words, I know not why, a slight shiver passed through me. She seemed to gain vitality and strength at every instant, but the chill of the great room struck into me more and more.

"She broke into a fantastic flow of spirits, clapping her hands, and dancing about me like a child. Who was she? And was I myself, or was she mocking me when she implied that we had belonged to each other of old? At length she stood still before me, crossing her hands over her breast. I saw upon the forefinger of her right hand the gleam of an antique ring.

" 'Where did you get that ring?' I demanded.

"She shook her head and laughed. 'Have you been faithful?' she asked. 'It is my ring; it is the ring that unites us; it is the ring you gave me when you loved me first. It is the ring of the Kern—the fairy ring, and I am your Ethelind—Ethelind Fionguala.'

" 'So be it,' I said, casting aside all doubt and fear, and yielding myself wholly to the spell of her inscrutable eyes and wooing lips. 'You are mine, and I am yours, and let us be happy while the hours last.'

" 'You are mine, and I am yours,' she repeated, nodding her head with an elfish smile. 'Come and sit beside me, and sing that sweet song again that you sang to me so long ago. Ah, now I shall live a hundred years.'

"We seated ourselves on the ottoman, and while she nestled luxuriously among the cushions, I took my banjo and sang to her. The song and the music resounded through the lofty room, and came back in throbbing echoes. And before me as I sang I saw the face and form of Ethelind Fionguala, in her jeweled bridal dress, gazing at me with burning eyes. She was pale no longer, but ruddy and warm, and life was like a flame within her. It was I who had become cold and bloodless, yet with the last life that was in me I would have sung to her of love that can never die. But at length my eyes grew dim, the room seemed to darken, the form of Ethelind alternately brightened and waxed indistinct, like the last flickerings of a fire; I swayed toward her, and felt myself lapsing into unconsciousness, with my head resting on her white shoulder."

Here Keningale paused a few moments in his story, flung a fresh log upon the fire, and then continued:

"I awoke, I know not how long afterward. I was in a vast, empty room in a ruined building. Rotten shreds of drapery depended from the walls, and heavy festoons of spiders' webs gray with dust covered the windows, which were destitute of glass or sash; they had been boarded up with rough planks which had themselves become rotten with age, and admitted through their holes and crevices pallid rays of light and chilly draughts of air. A bat, disturbed by these rays or by my own movement, detached himself from his hold on a remnant of moldy tapestry near me, and after circling dizzily around my head, wheeled the flickering noiselessness of his flight into a darker corner. As I arose unsteadily from the heap of miscellaneous rubbish on which I had been lying, something which had been resting across my knees fell to the floor with a rattle. I picked it up, and found it to be my banjo—as you see it now.

"Well, that is all I have to tell. My health was seriously impaired; all the blood seemed to have been drawn out of my veins; I was pale and haggard, and the chill—Ah, that chill," murmured Keningale, drawing nearer to the fire, and spreading out his hands to catch the warmth—"I shall never get over it; I shall carry it to my grave."

BODIES OF THE DEAD

Ambrose Bierce

That of Granny Magone.

About ten miles to the southeast of Whitesburg, Ky., in a little "cove" of the Cumberland mountains, lived for many years an old woman named Sarah (or Mary) Magone. Her house, built of logs and containing but two rooms, was a mile and a half distant from any other, in the wildest part of the "cove," entirely surrounded by forest except on one side, where a little field, or "patch," of about a half-acre served her for a vegetable garden. How she subsisted nobody exactly knew; she was reputed to be a miser with a concealed hoard; she certainly paid for what few articles she procured on her rare visits to the village store. Many of her ignorant neighbors believed her to be a witch, or thought, at least, that she possessed some kind of supernatural powers. In November, 1881, she died, and fortunately enough, the body was found while yet

197

warm by a passing hunter, who locked the door of the cabin and conveyed the news to the nearest settlement.

Several persons living in the vicinity at once went to the cabin to prepare for her burial; others were to follow the next day with a coffin and whatever else was needful. Among those who first went was the Rev. Elias Atney, a Methodist minister of Whitesburg, who happened to be in the neighborhood visiting a relation. He was to conduct the funeral services on the following day. Mr. Atney is, or was, well known in Whitesburg and all that country as a good and pious man of good birth and education. He was closely related to the Marshalls and several other families of distinction. It is from him that the particulars here related were learned; and the account is confirmed by the affidavits of John Hershaw, William C. Wrightman, and Catharine Doub, residents of the vicinity and eye-witnesses.

The body of "Granny" Magone had been "laid out" on a wide plank supported by two chairs at the end of the principal room, opposite the fireplace, and the persons mentioned were acting as "watchers," according to the local custom. A bright fire on the hearth lighted one end of the room brilliantly, the other dimly. The watchers sat about the fire, talking in subdued tones, when a sudden noise in the direction of the corpse caused them all to turn and look. In a black shadow near the remains, they saw two glowing eyes staring fixedly; and before they could do more than rise, uttering exclamations of alarm, a large black cat leaped upon the body and fastened its teeth into the cloth covering the face. Instantly the right hand of the dead was violently raised from the side, seized the cat, and hurled it against the wall, whence it fell to the floor, and then dashed wildly through an open window into the outer darkness, and was seen no more.

Inconceivably horrified, the watchers stood a moment speechless; but finally, with returning courage, approached the body. The face-cloth lay upon the floor; the cheek was terribly torn; the right arm hung stiffly over the side of the plank. There was not a sign of life. They chafed the forehead, the withered cheeks and neck. They carried the body to the heat of the fire and worked upon it for hours: all in vain. But the funeral was postponed until the fourth day brought unmistakable evidence of dissolution, and poor Granny was buried.

"Ah, but your eyes deceived you," said he to whom the reverend gentleman related the occurrence. "The arm was disturbed by the efforts of the cat, which, taking sudden fright, leaped blindly against the wall."

"No," he answered, "the clenched right hand, with its long nails, was full of black fur."

A Light Sleeper.

John Hoskin, living in San Francisco, had a beautiful wife, to whom he was devotedly attached. In the spring of 1871 Mrs. Hoskin went East to visit her relations in Springfield, Ill., where, a week after her arrival, she suddenly died of some disease of the heart; at least the physician said so. Mr. Hoskin was at once apprised of his loss, by telegraph, and he directed that the body be sent to San Francisco. On arrival there the metallic case containing the remains was opened. The body was lying on the right side, the right hand under the cheek, the other on the breast. The posture was the perfectly natural one of a sleeping child, and in a letter to the deceased lady's father, Mr. Martin L. Whitney of Springfield, Mr. Hoskin expressed a grateful sense of the thoughtfulness that had so composed the remains as to soften the suggestion of death. To his surprise he learned from the father that nothing of the kind had been done: the body had been put in the casket in the customary way, lying on the back, with the arms extended along the sides. In the meantime the casket had been deposited in the receiving vault at Laurel Hill Cemetery, awaiting the completion of a tomb.

Greatly disquieted by this revelation, Hoskin did not at once reflect that the easy and natural posture and placid expression precluded the idea of suspended animation, subsequent revival, and eventual death by suffocation. He insisted that his wife had been murdered by medical incompetency and heedless haste. Under the influence of this feeling he wrote to Mr. Whitney again, expressing in passionate terms his horror and renewed grief. Some days afterward, someone having suggested that the casket had been opened *en route*, probably in the hope of plunder, and pointing out the impossibility of the change having occurred in the straitened space of the confining metal, it was resolved to reopen it.

Removal of the lid disclosed a new horror: the body now lay upon its *left* side. The position was cramped, and to a living person would have been uncomfortable. The face wore an expression of pain. Some costly rings on the fingers were undisturbed. Overcome by his emotions, to which was now added a sharp, if mistaken remorse, Mr. Hoskin lost his reason, dying years afterward in the asylum at Stockton.

A physician having been summoned, to assist in clearing up the mystery, viewed the body of the dead woman, pronounced life obviously extinct, and ordered the casket closed for the third and last time. "Obviously extinct," indeed: the corpse had, in fact, been embalmed at Springfield.

The Mystery of Charles Farquharson.

One night in the summer of 1843 William Hayner Gordon, of Philadelphia, lay in his bed reading Goldsmith's "Traveler," by the light of a candle. It was about eleven o'clock. The room was in the third story of the house and had two windows looking out upon Chestnut Street; there was no balcony, nothing below the windows but other windows in a smooth brick wall.

Becoming drowsy, Gordon laid away his book, extinguished his candle, and composed himself to sleep. A moment later (as he afterward averred) he remembered that he had neglected to place his watch within reach, and rose in the dark to get it from the pocket of his waistcoat, which he had hung on the back of a chair on the opposite side of the room, near one of the windows. In crossing, his foot came in contact with some heavy object and he was thrown to the floor. Rising, he struck a match and lighted his candle. In the center of the room lay the corpse of a man.

Gordon was no coward, as he afterward proved by his gallant death upon the enemy's parapet at Chapultepec, but this strange apparition of a human corpse where but a moment before, as he believed, there had been nothing, was too much for his nerves, and he cried aloud. Henri Granier, who occupied an adjoining room, but had not retired, came instantly to Gordon's door and attempted to enter. The door being bolted, and Gordon too greatly agitated to open it, Granier burst it in.

Gordon was taken into custody and an inquest held, but what has been related was all that could be ascertained. The most diligent efforts on the part of the police and the press failed to identify the dead. Physicians testifying at the inquest agreed that death had occurred but a few hours before the discovery, but none was able to divine the cause; all the organs of the body were in

201

an apparently healthy condition; there were no traces of either violence or poison.

Eight or ten months later Gordon received a letter from Charles Ritcher in Bombay, relating the death in that city of Charles Farquharson, whom both Gordon and Ritcher had known when all were boys. Enclosed in the letter was a daguerreotype of the deceased, found among his effects. As nearly as the living can look like the dead it was an exact likeness of the mysterious body found in Gordon's bedroom, and it was with a strange feeling that Gordon observed that the death, making allowance for the difference of time, was said to have occurred on the very night of the adventure. He wrote for further particulars, with especial reference to what disposition had been made of Farquharson's body.

"You know he turned Parsee," wrote Ritcher in reply; "so his naked remains were exposed on the grating of the Tower of Silence, as those of all good Parsees are. I saw the buzzards fighting for them and gorging themselves helpless on his fragments."

On some pretense Gordon and his friends obtained authority to open the dead man's grave. The coffin had evidently not been disturbed. They unscrewed the lid. The shroud was a trifle moldy. There was no body nor any vestige of one.

Dead and "Gone."

On the morning of the 14th day of August, 1872, George J. Reid, a young man of twenty-one years, living at Xenia, O., fell while walking across the dining room on his father's house. The family consisted of his father, mother, two sisters, and a cousin, a boy of fifteen. All were present at the breakfast table. George entered the room, but instead of taking his accustomed seat near the door by which he had entered, passed it and went obliquely toward one of the windows—with what purpose no one knows. He had passed the table but a few steps when he fell heavily to the floor and did not again breathe. The body was carried into a bedroom and, after vain efforts at resuscitation by the stricken family, left lying on the bed with composed limbs and covered face.

In the meantime the boy had been hastily dispatched for a physician, who arrived some twenty minutes after the death. He afterward remembered as an uncommon circumstance that when he arrived the weeping relations—father, mother, and two sisters—were all in the room out of which the bedroom door opened, and that the door was closed. There was no other door to the bedroom. This door was at once opened by the father of the deceased, and as the physician passed through it he observed the dead man's clothing lying in a heap on the floor. He saw, too, the outlines of the body under the sheet that had been thrown over it; and the profile was plainly discernible under the face-cloth, clear-cut and sharp, as profiles of the dead seem always to be. He approached and lifted the cloth. There was nothing there. He pulled away the sheet. Nothing.

The family had followed him into the room. At this astonishing discovery—if so it may be called—they looked at one another, at the physician, at the bed, in speechless amazement, forgetting to weep. A moment later the three ladies required the physician's care. The father's condition was but little better; he stood in a stupor, muttering inarticulately and staring like an idiot.

Having restored the ladies to a sense of their surroundings, the physician went to the window—the only one the room had, opening upon a garden. It was locked on the inside with the usual fastening attached to the bottom bar of the upper sash and engaging with the lower.

No inquest was held—there was nothing to hold it on; but the physician and many others who were curious as to this occurrence made the most searching investigation into all the circumstances; all without result. George Reid was dead and "gone," and that is all that is known to this day.

A Cold Night.

The first day's battle at Stone River had been fought, resulting in disaster to the Federal army, which had been driven from its original ground at every point except its extreme left. The weary troops at this point lay behind a railway embankment to which they had retired, and which had served them during the last hours of the fight as a breastwork to repel repeated charges of the enemy. Behind the line the ground was open and rocky. Great bowlders lay about everywhere, and among them lay many of the Federal dead, where they had been carried out of the way. Before the embankment the dead of both armies lay more thickly, but they had not been disturbed.

Among the dead in the bowlders lay one whom nobody seemed to know—a Federal sergeant, shot directly in the center of the forehead. One of our surgeons, from idle curiosity, or possibly with a view to the amusement of a group of officers during a lull in the engagement (we needed something to divert our minds), had pushed his probe clean through the head. The body lay on its back, its chin in the air, and with straightened limbs, as rigid as steel; frost on its white face and in its beard and hair. Some Christian soul had covered it with a blanket, but when the night became pretty sharp a companion of the writer removed this, and we lay beneath it ourselves.

With the exception of our pickets, who had been posted well out in front of the embankment, every man lay silent. Conversation was forbidden; to have made a fire, or even struck a match to light a pipe would have been a grave offense. Stamping horses, moaning wounded—everything that made a noise had been sent to the rear; the silence was absolute. Those whom the chill prevented from sleeping nevertheless reclined as they shivered, or sat with their hands on their arms, suffering but making no sign. Everyone had lost friends, and all expected death on the morrow. These matters are mentioned to show the improbability of anyone going about during these solemn hours to commit a ghastly practical joke.

When the dawn broke the sky was still clear. "We shall have a warm day," the writer's companion whispered as we rose in the gray light; "let's give back the poor devil his blanket."

The sergeant's body lay in the same place, two yards away. But not in the same attitude. It was upon its right side. The knees were drawn up nearly to the breast, both hands thrust to the wrist between the buttons of the jacket, the collar of which was turned up, concealing the ears. The shoulders were elevated, the head was retracted, the chin rested on the collar bone. The posture was that of one suffering from intense cold. But for what had been previously observed—but for the ghastly evidence of the bullet-hole—one might have thought the man had died of cold.

BODIES OF THE DEAD

A Creature of Habit.

At Hawley's Bar, a mining camp near Virginia City, Mont., a gambler named Henry Graham, but commonly known as "Gray Hank," met a miner named Dreyfuss one day, with whom he had had a dispute the previous night about a game of cards, and asked him into a barroom to have a drink. The unfortunate miner, taking this as an overture of peace, gladly accepted. They stood at the counter, and while Dreyfuss was in the act of drinking Graham shot him dead. This was in 1865. Within an hour after the murder Graham was in the hands of the vigilantes, and that evening at sunset, after a fair, if informal, trial, he was hanged to the limb of a tree which grew upon a little eminence within sight of the whole camp. The original intention had been to "string him up," as is customary in such affairs; and with a view to that operation the long rope had been thrown over the limb, while a dozen pairs of hands were ready to hoist away. For some reason this plan was abandoned; the free end of the rope was made fast to a bush and the victim compelled to stand on the back of a horse, which at the cut of a whip sprang from under him, leaving him swinging. When steadied, his feet were about eighteen inches from the earth.

The body remained suspended for exactly half an hour, the greater part of the crowd remaining about it: then the "judge" ordered it taken down. The rope was untied from the bush, and two men stood by to lower away. The moment the feet came squarely upon the ground the men engaged in lowering, thinking doubtless that those standing about the body had hold of it to support it, let go the rope. The body at once ran quickly forward toward the main part of the crowd, the rope paying out as it went. The head rolled from side to side, the eyes and tongue protruding, the face ghastly purple, the lips covered with bloody froth. With cries of horror the crowd ran hither and thither, stumbling, falling over one another, cursing. In and out among them—over the fallen, coming into collision with others, the horrible dead man "pranced," his feet lifted so high at each step that his knees struck his breast, his tongue swinging like that of a panting dog, the foam flying in flakes from his swollen lips. The deepening twilight added its terror to the scene, and men fled from the spot, not daring to look behind.

Straight into this confusion from the outskirts of the crowd walked with rapid steps the tall figure of a man whom all who saw instantly recognized as a master spirit. This was Dr. Arnold Spier, who with two other physicians had pronounced the man dead and had been returning to the camp. He moved as directly toward the dead man as the now somewhat less rapid and erratic movements of the latter would permit, and seized him in his arms. Encouraged by this, a score of men sprang shouting to the free end of the rope, which had not been drawn entirely over the limb, and laid hold of it, intending to make a finish of their work. They ran with it toward the bush to which it had been fastened, but there was no resistance; the physician had cut it from the murderer's neck. In a moment the body was lying on its back, with composed limbs and face upturned to the kindling stars, in the motionless rigidity appropriate to death. The hanging had been done well enough—the neck was broken.

"The dead are creatures of habit," said Dr. Spier. "A corpse which when on its feet will walk and run will lie still when placed on its back."

BERENICE

Edgar Allan Poe

Dicebant mihi sodales, si sepulchrum amicæ visitarem,
curas meas aliquantulum fore levatas.—*Ebn Zaiat.*

M isery is manifold. The wretchedness of earth is
multiform. Overarching the wide horizon as
the rainbow, its hues are as various as the hues
of that arch, as distinct too, yet as intimately blended.
Overarching the wide horizon as the rainbow! How is it
that from beauty I have derived a type of unloveliness?
from the covenant of peace a simile of sorrow? But as
in ethics, evil is a consequence of good, so in fact, out
of joy is sorrow born. Either the memory of the past
bliss is the anguish of to-day, or the agonies which *are*
have their origin in the ecstasies which *might have
been.*

My baptismal name is Egæus, that of my family I
will not mention. Yet there are no towers in the land
more time-honoured than my gloomy, grey, hereditary

halls. Our line has been called a race of visionaries; and in many striking particulars—in the character of the family mansion, in the frescoes of the chief saloon, in the tapestries of the dormitories, in the chiselling of some buttresses in the armoury, but more especially in the gallery of antique paintings, in the fashion of the library chamber, and lastly, in the very peculiar nature of the library's contents—there is more than sufficient evidence to warrant the belief.

The recollections of my earliest years are connected with that chamber, and with its volumes—of which latter I will say no more. Here died my mother. Herein was I born. But it is mere idleness to say that I had not lived before—that the soul has no previous existence. You deny it—let us not argue the matter. Convinced myself, I seek not to convince. There is, however, a remembrance of aerial forms—of spiritual and meaning eyes—of sounds, musical yet sad; a remembrance which will not be excluded; a memory like a shadow—vague, variable, indefinite, unsteady; and like a shadow, too, in the impossibility of my getting rid of it while the sunlight of my reason shall exist.

In that chamber was I born. Thus awaking from the long night of what seemed, but was not, nonentity, at once into the very regions of fairy land—into a palace of imagination—into the wild dominions of monastic thought and erudition—it is not singular that I gazed around me with a startled and ardent eye—that I loitered away my boyhood in books, and dissipated my youth in revery; but it *is* singular, that as years rolled away, and the noon of manhood found me still in the mansion of my fathers—it *is* wonderful what a stagnation there fell upon the springs of my life—wonderful how total an inversion took place in the character of my commonest thought. The realities of the world affected me as visions, and as visions only, while the wild ideas of the land of dreams became, in turn, not the material of my every-day existence, but in very deed that existence utterly and solely in itself.

Berenice and I were cousins, and we grew up together in my paternal halls. Yet different we grew—I, ill of health, and buried in gloom—she, agile, graceful, and overflowing with energy; her's the ramble on the hill-side—mine, the studies of the cloister; I, living within my own heart, and addicted, body and soul, to the most intense and painful meditation—she, roaming carelessly through life, with no thought of the shadows in her path, or the silent flight of the raven-winged hours. Berenice!—I call upon her name—Berenice!—and from the gray ruins of memory a thousand tumultuous recollections are startled at the sound! Ah, vividly is her image before me now, as in the early days of her light-heartedness and joy! Oh, gorgeous yet fantastic beauty! Oh, sylph amid the shrubberies of Arnheim! Oh, naiad among its fountains! And then—then all is mystery and terror, and a tale which should not be told. Disease—a fatal disease, fell like the simoom upon her frame; and even, while I gazed upon her, the spirit of change swept over her, pervading her mind, her habits and her character, and, in a manner the most subtle and terrible, disturbing even the identity of her person! Alas! the destroyer came and went!—and the victim—where is she! I knew her not—or knew her no longer as Berenice!

Among the numerous train of maladies superinduced by that fatal and primary one which effected a revolution of so horrible a kind in the moral and physical being of my cousin, may be mentioned as the most distressing and obstinate in its nature, a species of epilepsy not unfrequently terminating in *trance* itself— trance very nearly resembling positive dissolution, and from which her manner of recovery was, in most instances, startlingly abrupt. In the meantime, my own disease—for I have been told that I should call it by no other appellation—my own disease, then, grew rapidly upon me, and assumed finally a monomaniac character of a novel and extraordinary form—hourly and momently gaining vigor—and at length obtaining over me the most incomprehensible ascendency. This monomania, if I must so term it, consisted in a morbid irritability of those properties of the mind in metaphysical science termed the *attentive*. It is more than probable that I am not understood; but I fear, indeed, that it is in no manner possible to convey to the mind of the merely general reader, an adequate idea of that nervous *intensity of interest* with which, in my case, the powers of meditation (not to speak technically) busied and buried themselves, in the contemplation of even the most ordinary objects of the universe.

To muse for long unwearied hours, with my attention riveted to some frivolous device on the margin or in the typography of a book; to become absorbed, for the better part of a summer's day, in a quaint shadow falling aslant upon the tapestry or upon the floor; to lose myself, for an entire night, in watching the steady flame of a lamp, or the embers of a fire, to dream away whole days over the perfume of a flower; to repeat, monotonously, some common word, until the sound, by dint of frequent repetition, ceased to convey any idea whatever to the mind; to lose all sense of motion or physical existence, by means of absolute bodily quiescence long and obstinately persevered in: such were a few of the most common and least pernicious vagaries induced by a condition of the mental faculties, not, indeed, altogether unparalleled, but certainly bidding defiance to any thing like analysis or explanation.

Yet let me not be misapprehended. The undue, earnest, and morbid attention thus excited by objects in their own nature frivolous, must not be confounded in character with that ruminating propensity common to all mankind, and more especially indulged in by persons of ardent imagination. It was not even, as might be at first supposed, an extreme conditions, or exaggeration of such propensity, but primarily and essentially distinct and different. In the one instance, the dreamer, or enthusiast, being interested by an object usually *not* frivolous, imperceptibly loses sight of this object in a wilderness of deductions and suggestions issuing therefrom, until, at the conclusion of a day-dream *often replete with luxury*, he finds the *incitamentum*, or first cause of his musings, entirely vanished and forgotten. In my case, the primary object was *invariably frivolous*, although assuming, through the medium of my distempered vision, a refracted and unreal importance. Few deductions, if any, were made; and those few pertinaciously returning in upon the original object as a centre. The meditations were *never* pleasureable; and, at the termination of the revery, the first cause, so far from being out of sight, had attained that supernaturally exaggerated interest which was the prevailing feature of the disease. In a word, the powers of mind more particularly exercised were, with me, as I have said before, the *attentive*, and are, with the day-dreamer, the *speculative*.

My books, at this epoch, if they did not actually serve to irritate the disorder, partook, it will be perceived, largely, in their imaginative and inconsequential nature, of the characteristic qualities of the disorder itself. I well remember, among others, the treatise of the noble Italian, Coelius Secundus Curio, *"De Amplitudine Beati Regni Dei"*; St. Augustin's great work, "The City of God"; and Tertullian's *"De Carne Christi,"* in which the paradoxical sentence, *"Mortuus est Dei filius; credibile est quia ineptum est; et sepultus resurrexit;*

certum est quia impossible est," occupied my undivided time, for many weeks of laborious and fruitless investigation.

Thus it will appear that, shaken from its balance only by trivial things, my reason bore resemblance to that ocean-crag spoken of by Ptolemy Hephestion, which steadily resisting the attacks of human violence, and the fiercer fury of the waters and the winds, trembled only to the touch of the flower called Asphodel. And although, to a careless thinker, it might appear a matter beyond doubt, that the alteration produced by her unhappy malady, in the *moral* condition of Berenice, would afford me many objects for the exercise of that intense and abnormal meditation whose nature I have been at some trouble in explaining, yet such was not in any degree the case. In the lucid intervals of my infirmity, her calamity, indeed, gave me pain, and, taking deeply to heart that total wreck of her fair and gentle life, I did not fail to ponder, frequently and bitterly, upon the wonder-working means by which so strange a revolution had been so suddenly brought to pass. But these reflections partook not of the idiosyncrasy of my disease, and were such as would have occurred, under similar circumstances, to the ordinary mass of mankind. True to its own character, my disorder revelled in the less important but more startling changes wrought in the *physical* frame of Berenice—in the singular and most appalling distortion of her personal identity.

During the brightest days of her unparalleled beauty, most surely I had never loved her. In the strange anomaly of my existence, feelings with me, *had never been* of the heart, and my passions *always were* of the mind. Through the gray of the early morning—among the trellised shadows of the forest at noonday—and in the silence of my library at night—she had flitted by my eyes, and I had seen her—not as the living and breathing Berenice, but as the Berenice of a dream; not as a being of the earth, earthly, but as the abstraction of such a being; not as a thing to admire, but to analyze; not as an object of love, but as the theme of the most abstruse although desultory speculation. And *now*—now I shuddered in her presence, and grew pale at her approach; yet, bitterly lamenting her fallen and desolate condition, I called to mind that she had loved me long, and, in an evil moment, I spoke to her of marriage.

And at length the period of our nuptials was approaching, when, upon an afternoon in the winter of the year—one of those unseasonably warm, calm, and misty days which are the nurse of the beautiful Halcyon,*—I sat (and sat, as I thought, alone) in the inner apartment of the library. But uplifting my eyes, I saw that Berenice stood before me.

Was it my own excited imagination—or the misty influence of the atmosphere—or the uncertain twilight of the chamber—or the gray draperies which fell around her figure—that caused in it so vacillating and indistinct an outline? I could not tell. She spoke no word; and I—not for words could I have uttered a syllable. An icy chill ran through my frame; a sense of insufferable anxiety oppressed me; a consuming curiosity pervaded my soul; and, sinking back upon the chair, I remained for some time breathless and motionless, with my eyes riveted upon her person. Alas! its emaciation was excessive, and not one vestige of the former being lurked in any single line of the contour. My burning glances at length fell upon the face.

The forehead was high, and very pale, and singularly placid; and the once jetty hair fell partially over it, and

---

*For as Jove, during the winter season, gives twice seven days of warmth, men have called this element and temperate time the nurse of the beautiful Halcyon.—*Simonides.*

overshadowed the hollow temples with innumerable ringlets, now of a vivid yellow, and jarring discordantly, in their fantastic character, with the reigning melancholy of the countenance. The eyes were lifeless, and lustreless, and seemingly pupilless, and I shrank involuntarily from their glassy stare to the contemplation of the thin and shrunken lips. They parted; and in a smile of peculiar meaning, *the teeth* of the changed Berenice disclosed themselves slowly to my view. Would to God that I had never beheld them, or that, having done so, I had died!

The shutting of a door disturbed me, and looking up, I found that my cousin had departed from the chamber. But from the disordered chamber of my brain, had not, alas! departed, and would not be driven away, the white and ghastly *spectrum* of the teeth. Not a speck on their surface—not a shade on their enamel—not an indenture in their edges—but what the brief period of her smile had sufficed to brand in upon my memory. I saw them *now* even more unequivocally than I beheld them *then*. The teeth!—the teeth!—they were here, and there, and everywhere, and visibly and palpably before me; long, narrow, and excessively white, with the pale lips writhing about them, as in the very moment of their first terrible development. Then came the full fury of my *monomania*, and I struggled in vain against its strange and irresistible influence. In the multiplied objects of the external world I had no thoughts but for the teeth. For these I longed with a frenzied desire. All other matters and all different interests became absorbed in their single contemplation. They—they alone were present to the mental eye, and they, in their sole individuality, became the essence of my mental life. I held them in every light. I turned them in every attitude. I surveyed their characteristics. I dwelt upon their peculiarities. I pondered upon their conformation. I mused upon the alteration in their nature. I shuddered as I assigned to them, in imagination, a sensitive and sentient power, and even when unassisted by the lips, a capability of moral expression. Of Mademoiselle Salle it has been well said: *"Que tous ses pas etaient des sentiments,"* and of Berenice I more seriously believed *que tous ses dents etaient des idees. Des idees!*—ah, here was the idiotic thought that destroyed me! *Des idees!*—ah, *therefore* it was that I coveted them so madly! I felt that their possession could alone ever restore me to peace, in giving me back to reason.

And the evening closed in upon me thus—and then the darkness came, and tarried, and went—and the day again dawned—and the mists of a second night were now gathering around—and still I sat motionless in that solitary room—and still I sat buried in meditation—and still the *phantasma* of the teeth maintained its terrible ascendancy, as, with the most vivid and hideous distinctness, it floated about amid the changing lights and shadows of the chamber. At length there broke in upon my dreams a cry as of horror and dismay; and thereunto, after a pause, succeeded the sound of troubled voices, intermingled with many low moanings of sorrow or of pain. I arose from my seat, and throwing open one of the doors of the library, saw standing out in the antechamber a servant maiden, all in tears, who told me that Berenice was—no more! She had been seized with epilepsy in the early morning, and now, at the closing in of the night, the grave was ready for its tenant, and all the preparations for the burial were completed.

I found myself sitting in the library, and again sitting there alone. It seemed to me that I had newly awakened from a confused and exciting dream. I knew that it was now midnight, and I was well aware, that since the setting of the sun, Berenice had been interred. But of that dreary period which intervened I had no positive, at least no definite, comprehension. Yet its memory was replete with horror—horror more horrible from being vague, and terror more terrible from ambiguity. It was a fearful page in the record of my existence, written all over with dim, and hideous, and unintelligible recollections. I strived to decipher them, but in vain; while ever and anon, like the spirit of a departed sound, the shrill and piercing shriek of a female voice seemed to be ringing in my ears. I had done a deed—what was it? I asked myself the question aloud, and the whispering echoes of the chamber answered me—*"What was it?"*

On the table beside me burned a lamp, and near it lay a little box. It was of no remarkable character, and I had seen it frequently before, for it was the property of the family physician; but how came it *there*, upon my table, and why did I shudder in regarding it. These things were in no manner to be accounted for, and my eyes at length dropped to the open pages of a book, and to a sentence underscored therein. The words were the singular but simple ones of the poet Ebn Zaiat:—*"Dicebant mihi sodales si sepulchrum amicæ visitarem, curas meas aliquantulum fore levatas."* Why, then, as I perused them, did the hairs of my head erect themselves on end, and the blood of my body become congealed within my veins?

There came a light tap at the library door—and, pale as the tenant of a tomb, a menial entered upon tiptoe. His looks were wild with terror, and he spoke to me in a voice tremulous, husky and very low. What said he?—some broken sentences I heard. He told of a wild cry disturbing the silence of the night—of the gathering together of the household—of a search in the direction of the sound; and then his tones grew thrillingly distinct as he whispered me of a violated grave—of a disfigured

body enshrouded, yet still breathing—still palpitating—
still alive!

He pointed to my garments; they were muddy and clotted with gore. I spoke not, and he took me gently by the hand: it was indented with the impress of human nails. He directed my attention to some object against the wall. I looked at it for some minutes: it was a spade. With a shriek I bounded to the table, and grasped the box that lay upon it. But I could not force it open; and, in my tremor, it slipped from my hands, and fell heavily, and burst into pieces; and from it, with a rattling sound, there rolled out some instruments of dental surgery, intermingled with thirty-two small, white, and ivory-looking substances that were scattered to and fro about the floor.